Gabriel

Only one gets out alive.

By Mike Evans

Editor and Proofreader Torchbearer Editing Services
Original edit Veronica Smith and Rosa Thomas-Mcbroom
Cover art by David Mickolas

Dedications: I would like to thank my wife, Emily, and my kids for allowing me the time to pursue my dreams. I love each of you more than anything! I would like to thank all of my friends and fans that I have gotten to know over the last year; it has been a wonderful experience and I have felt supported like never before because of it!

Please look for me on Facebook

Mike's Newsletter sign up
http://tinyurl.com/evansnewsletter

Mike Evans Fan Club Page Facebook
https://www.facebook.com/groups/1523345561293296

M. Evans' Author Page on Facebook
https://www.facebook.com/pages/M-Evans-Author/1438259789750360

Mike Evans Author Website
http://mevansm01.wix.com/mikeevansauthor

Contact Email
m.evansauthor@gmail.com

Mike Evans on Amazon
http://www.amazon.com/Mike-Evans/e/B00IQ9Z75A

Books by Mike Evans

The Orphans Series
The Orphans: Origins Vol I
Surviving the Turned Vol II (The Orphans Series)
Strangers Vol III (The Orphans Series)
White Lie Vol IV (The Orphans Series)
Civil War Vol V (The Orphans Series)

Gabriel Series
Gabriel: Only one gets out alive
Pitch Black (Gabriel Book 2)
Body Count (Gabriel Book 3)

The Uninvited Series
The Uninvited Book I
The Stranger Book II of The Uninvited series
The Unwelcomed Book III of The Uninvited series coming soon

Buried: Broken oaths

Demons Beware

This is the story of Gabriel.
Bullets don't have a preference. They do not know if they're going into the pure of heart or the depths of Satan's evil. Bullets make no choices and have no control. It is the keeper of the trigger that makes the decision.

Chapter 1
Broken Promises

May 2018, Operation Homebound

The sun had been down for hours in the South American jungle. The warm tropical climate was still making the temperature hot enough to be miserable. Gabriel wiped at his brow as the sweat poured from every pore on his body. It was making his gear feel at least thirty pounds heavier. The face paint that he used to camouflage his face and scalp with was just another thing to retain the body heat.

He stopped trudging through the forest and stared up into a wooded canopy that stretched into a heaven he did not believe in. He reached over his shoulder and took a small tube from his camel pack and drank a few small sips. Gabriel set his high-powered, long-range rifle against one of the trees. He listened for a moment, hearing the strangers of the night screaming their wild cries into the darkness. Their echoes engulfed everything around him.

He stared curiously into the dark ahead. At first, he dismissed what he was seeing. It seemed unreal, the images making no sense. But after he saw it steadily for a few minutes, he gave it his undivided attention. Gabriel could just barely make out a light that seemed to glow brighter every second. He realized what he was staring at was the gentle glow of the end of a cigarette. No self-respecting sniper would have a cigarette in the middle of the night if they knew what they were doing and wanted to come back out of the massive jungle.

Gabriel reached for his sniper rifle and melted back into the trees. He became one with the ground before trying to get eyes on the smoker in the distance. He closed his eyes and when he opened them, he saw with fresh eyes exactly what he thought he would and so much more.

Gabriel breathed easy, staring at his perimeter in front of him. He counted four men and could have not been more pleased to see that they were soldiers and not fellow snipers or hitters like himself. He was less than a mile from his assignment, where he'd dig into a sniper nest until his target came out. If he didn't come out, he would do everything he could to get into the fortress.

As he closed the distance to within fifty yards, his leg started vibrating unexpectedly. He stopped his approach, pulled out a satellite phone, and punched the talk button. He brought it up to his ear, listening. When no voice said anything, Gabriel—who was usually able to wait forever—said, "I'm sure you called for a reason, didn't you?"

A much older man on the other end cleared his throat, trying to preserve every second he could before he had to speak to Gabriel. He said, "Son, you're speaking to a superior commanding officer. I hope you realize that, son."

"I'm fifty yards from a kill, sir. You are compromising my position, my kill, and my life. So I'm sorry if I come off as impatient. I have pending circumstances that I feel are more important than this call. But blame me because I am the dumbshit that answered the fucking phone call. I should have disobeyed orders and just turned the phone off completely. But we both know how that is."

"I called with a purpose. Although, having a 'come to Jesus meeting' about you and your damn respect for authority needs to be addressed, son. Hell, I think that I'm going to move it to the top of my fucking to-do list. I'll get to tell the great Gabriel that, no matter how important he is, we need to understand a common respect for one another."

"Yeah, that sounds like a great conversation… but really, what's the point of calling? You are just going to get me killed if I don't move forward."

"The reason for my call is to tell you to back out of there and get back to your extraction point along the river."

"How long until I get a ride? What's the reason for the

extraction?"

"You have two days, or you are going to have to make it out of South America on your own."

"Sir, it took me five days to get in, and there wasn't any fucking around trying to get here. I walked, climbed, and slid. Then I went through shit that textbooks do not understand to get my ass in here."

"Watch your mouth, soldier!"

"You fucking watch it, sir. You just told me to abandon my mission and told me that I'm a dead man. It would be impossible to make that kind of trip. I could sprint the entire way and still not make it in enough time."

"Son, it's out of our hands. Our informant was captured and we think he talked."

Gabriel sat staring into the distance; the four men did not know that the seconds they had left on earth were precious ones. He looked further into the distance, making sure that four men really were all that was left and that no stragglers had made their way in.

"I'm not leaving that man in there to be tortured because one of your guys probably offered him a year's pay to give up intel that would easily get him killed. He was just trying to do right by his family and probably didn't believe the South American drug cartel was the almighty. You do realize that the drug lords here will kill everyone that he's ever met, right? If they haven't done so already."

"That's a compelling speech, kid, but the man made up his mind. No one forced him to do anything"

"Yeah, amazing that a dirt-poor man would reach out and grab a lotto ticket, even if it was on fire."

"Regardless of whether he made a good decision or not, Gabriel, you need to leave now. If you do, we might be able to bribe your ride with enough that you'll have the time you need to get to your rendezvous point."

"You tell them they wait, no matter what. I can get Raul from in there and be on our way in less than an hour.

And I can take out the main target while I'm in there."

"Gabriel, you leave and you do it now! That's an order! Those men only care about money, but they value their lives over that, son."

"They leave, and I'll hunt down every last one of them and slit their throats. Do you understand that? They've met me; they know that I can and will."

"That isn't how we operate, and you know it, kid."

"I stopped being a kid a long god damn time ago. If you can't control your assets, then maybe you ought to be looking into some new ones."

"So, you're saying that you'll risk your life for some damn—"

"No, I'm not risking my life for him or anyone else. I've been in the shit for days now and I'm going to finish my mission. But when I'm done—and I will be done, I promise you that—you better not plan on a debriefing. I'm out after this. God knows there are enough job offers out there for someone with a special skill set like mine."

"I think you need to stop and think about this Jacob."

"Don't call me that when I'm working. If someone listened to this radio chatter, they could figure a lot out if you used my last name."

"I think you should come in, Gabriel. We can give you some time off, some time to get your head back in the game, to get set back up in the righteous path that you are taking."

"God! Could you be more full of yourself? I am going to take a vacation, and it's going to be a long one after I get out of this damn place. But I'm out after this, Tony. I'm sick of this shit. You have a billion dollars' worth of intel in your budget and I'm trekking through a damn jungle by myself with little more than a rifle and a handgun."

Tony yelled, "Hey, we can change, kid; we can do something else! Just tell us what you want. Hell, you plan your own ops; maybe you'll get some management under your belt, take on some kids out of training, and teach them how to do some of those wonderful things that you do."

"I'm out, Tony. I'm finishing this; that's it and then I am done."

"You don't decide when you quit. You know that we have other people trained right, Gabriel? We can bring you in."

"You could try and bring me in. I don't have anything personal against you, Tony. I know you are doing what you think you need to do, but if you send anyone after me, you can cross those men off of your list. I promise you that."

"Why don't you take some time to think, son. Let's talk about this again in a couple weeks once you make it back."

"Goodbye, Tony."

Gabriel hit the end button on the satellite phone and slid it back into his pocket. He took a long, deep breath and cracked his neck from side to side. He pulled out his silenced handgun and a knife and closed the distance as quietly and quickly as he could. Time was already something to be worried about, and now he had even less of it than before. He started his approach again and once he made it halfway there, he picked up a rock and threw it into the distance. The men snapped their heads around, and three of them ran in that direction, screaming in Portuguese.

One man stood point, making sure a second gunman did not come through that they did not know about. Gabriel moved through the distance, waiting for the three men to be far enough out of sight that they would not see the fourth man's ending. Gabriel tossed one last rock twenty yards to the man's right. When he turned his head, Gabriel stepped out of the shadows, gripped the man's rifle with his left hand, and quickly stabbed him in the lungs, thigh, and neck with his right hand. The man was already dead before the pain had time to register in his body. It happened so quickly that he was unable to muster a scream.

Gabriel hung him from a tree branch sticking out of

the trunk, giving the appearance that he was still very much alive. Gabriel patted the man down, taking his radio and his cigarettes, lighting one, and letting it hang from his lips. He placed it out of the side of the man's mouth so the blood coming from it would not put it out. He backed up, waiting in the shadows and letting the men circle around. When they found nothing, they came back and yelled to the man who was hung up in the tree. Gabriel had learned enough Portuguese to get him by. The leader of the group yelled, "Carlos, what are you doing standing there? You should be walking around making sure that government piece of shit is not lurking in the shadows."

They watched as the man lifted his rifle and pointed it directly at them. The three started screaming at him to put it down—to lower the weapon. They started firing when their man would not listen. Gabriel unleashed the machine gun on the three of them. The shots echoed throughout the jungle as the bodies fell, one after another. Gabriel made his way to the edge of the woods after quickly covering the men with brush. He was set to make his way to the compound, when he thought about his escape from the jungle and how a ride would be useful.

Gabriel pulled out his satellite phone and dialed a private number. It rang five times and as he was about to put it down, cursing his handler, Tony Baker, a voice came over the phone. "You must be one special bastard if you got this number; not many do. Who do I have the pleasure of speaking with on this beautiful, tropical, alcohol-induced day?"

"It's Gabriel. I need a ride, Forsyth, and I need it now. It's important."

The man got serious. "Well, what's so important about it?"

"It means my life and the life of one of my assets that was captured. I need you to get that Widow Maker in the air and get on your way here, and I need you to do it now. Are you available for pickup and transport?"

Back in Panama, Forsyth looked at the pool in front of him and spun the umbrella in his drink around slowly while staring at one of the locals and what she thought passed for a bikini. He waved a giant mitt of a hand at her. She smiled back, trying to take the man seriously, in his cargo shorts and red Hawaiian shirt. She waved, and he raised his eyebrows at her. "I'm having a pretty good time right now. I think if I play my cards right, and I'm willing to spend a hundred bucks, I may have the most memorable half hour of my life with a beauty that is half my age."

"No shit, you are in Panama? I'm just a few jumps down to Manaus, Brazil. Do you think you can get down here in two days?"

"I'd have to leave in the next couple hours, but I have bad news for you on that."

"Tick-tock, Forsyth."

"It's gonna cost you about ten thousand to get you out of there. I have a pretty big week planned down here. I'd have to cancel a few jobs."

"You go to Panama to fuck, not work; you and I both know that."

"Well, that may or may not be true, but I do have some stuff lined up and…"

"Cut the shit. I'll wire you five grand when you come get me. You can also mark down that I will owe you a solid favor at some point in the future. This, of course, is the kind of help that you and I both know is worth much more than the five grand you are passing up on."

Forsyth sat staring at the young woman, thinking that even if he accepted, he had plenty of time to get to know her a little better. He figured as long as he called ahead and asked to have the Widow Maker fueled and prepped in advance, there was plenty of time. He wrote down the city, slammed his drink, and said, "Yeah, you got it, Gabriel, but you're going to owe me a big fucking favor."

Gabriel was already regretting starting his solo career in the debt of another but reluctantly said, "Yeah, I'm aware of what I'm going to have to do. You just make sure you get as close as you can. We should be there early, so don't fuck around."

"Would I do that?"

"Yes, yes you would. So, make sure you get wheels in the air in the next few hours. I'm out, and thanks." Gabriel hit the end button, always believing in hanging up the phone when he had gotten the answer that he wanted. He put the phone back in his pants pocket, knowing it might mean life or death if he lost it.

He took a long, deep breath and placed a silencer on his high-powered rifle, knowing that he was going to have to use it for more than one shot. He knew that there would be multiple men and multiple kills because there was no way he would be fortunate enough to get the shot he needed to take out the main target. Gabriel had been in situations similar to this where the target was bunkered down and locked up tight. The man would not leave his safe place until the men he sent into the woods had captured or killed the intruder.

He pulled off his pack, took a few items out of it, and hid it inside a dead tree trunk. He then ran with everything he had in his legs, which for Gabriel was quite a lot. Two minutes later, he dived down into the deep grass. A fireball erupted in the jungle, setting the trees and canopy ablaze. The light from it was bright enough that it lit up a perimeter thirty yards wide around the jungle's edge.

The sirens went off in the compound, and men in trucks came flying out of the gates. The trucks had large floodlights attached to the top and they swung left to right as they drove, looking for a target. Gabriel army-crawled as fast as he could, until he was halfway between the compound and the jungle's edge. He waited an extra minute for the men to get there. He counted five men in the truck—five that he knew would never come back. He hit a detonator button, unleashing a second string of explosions along the edge of the jungle. These were much more dangerous than the first explosions and incinerated the group of men. They ran into the field screaming in horror, their skin melting from the napalm that the bomb had in it.

Gabriel scanned the top of the compound, spotting the guard towers where two men were scanning the field and jungle in front of them. The binoculars they were using were lit red as they searched, using thermal heat signatures. The men were using them in all directions to get a visual confirmation on Gabriel. Gabriel sent two bullets, one for each man, traveling across the field. The bullets shattered the guard tower's glass and knocked each man backwards, stumbling out of the back and to the ground below. If the bullet had not already killed them, they would have died instantly from a broken neck.

Gabriel got up, running in a crouched position as quickly as he could while staying as low as possible. He kept his rifle slung and ran with his mini assault rifle fully extended and ready to kill. He scanned the distance in front of him, making sure that if he was looking at it, that he was aiming at it. He could remember his instructor, Clary, from week one at training screaming at the top of his lungs. *"By god, son, if you don't raise that fucking rifle, I am going to take it from you and insert it in your ass!"*

He shook the voice of his instructor out of his head, but not the lessons. Gabriel made his way near the entrance, moving one slow step at a time until he was at the gate. He pulled a pair of wire cutters from his pocket and made a hole large enough that he could slip under. Gabriel made his way to the building's entrance and used a mirror to look around the corner without having to make his head a target. Gabriel knew that there was little chance that the space was going to be unoccupied.

He pulled two smoke grenades from his belt, ripping the pin out of each of them. He tossed them into the courtyard, one close and the other towards the back of the open space. He slipped on a gas mask and bounced in place, giving it a ten second count to let the smoke fill the space. Gabriel ducked low, crouched, and flipped down his second set of eyes. He hit the power switch, seeing everything in thermal heat signatures. He ran along the edge of the inside, firing silenced shots. He took men out in a calculated, cool technique, making sure that nothing was alive by the time he was done. When there was no one left to kill, he moved inside the building. Gabriel checked his watch, knowing damn well that he was going to need to move quickly. He wasn't quite sure what he would do if they had broken the legs of the asset.

Gabriel walked through the hall. He would have never found the man if it hadn't been for the agonizing screams of pain coming from the around the corner of a very long hallway. Gabriel walked quickly, staying down. He didn't see any security cameras and he smiled briefly. The drug lords always thought that their gates were impenetrable and therefore their inner space secure.

Gabriel got to the end of the corner and looked around quickly. He didn't hesitate when another scream erupted. This scream was a long-lasting, blood-curdling scream. He sprinted for the doorway, pulled a flash-bang grenade, and tossed it through. Gabriel's optimism went up when he looked in and saw Alejandro Sonra, the head of this cartel and architect of their cocaine infrastructure, standing over Raul with a makeshift weapon that he looked like he'd been using. It had two small sticks with a metal wire between the two. The wire was dripping with blood and on the ground were four fingers that could only have come off of Raul's left hand.

The men saw Gabriel moving across the front of the torture room like a ghost, but they were too slow. They heard the clinking of the grenade skidding across the floor and screams of "granada, granada, down down!" They were too late as it detonated, blinding and sending them into a disorientation like they'd never known. Gabriel moved in through the smoke, picturing where they had been in his mind, and where their hunched-over forms on the ground would be.

He found the first man and slammed a knee into his face and when his head snapped up Gabriel slit his throat. Then with a second strike, he sent the knife up under his chin, finishing him. The second man ran towards Gabriel still coughing, but knew that his life was over if he did not do something about the gringo that had run through the door, killing without asking questions. It went without saying that he would be next. He screamed his war cry, letting Gabriel know he was coming. He swung a machete at a straight down arch on Gabriel who was keeping low. Gabriel caught it with his left hand and sliced at the man's wrist with his knife, causing him to drop the machete. Then, using a two-hand assist, he plunged the knife into the man's chest, cutting down and pulling with everything he had, splitting him from chest to pelvic. The man's watering eyes were already dead before his guts emptied out onto the floor.

The leader of the group tried pulling his pistol as his last man was gutted like a pig. Gabriel brought his arm up over his head with practiced perfection and threw his knife, embedding it into the man's throat. He gripped it with both hands and watched as Gabriel made his path through the room, coming out of the smoke towards him, placed a silenced handgun next to his head, and fired a single shot. Alejandro fell to the ground hard where his blood pooled on the white tiled floor.

Raul was screaming at the top of his lungs, "Nenhum fantasma! Shoot nenhum fantasma... shoot!"

Gabriel made a calming motion with his hands and whispered, "I'm not going to shoot you and I am not a ghost."

The man asked, "Você é o diabo?"

Gabriel cut the man loose, shrugging at that question. He said, "Para aqueles que o pecado." *Only to those that have sinned.* The man nodded, making the sign of the cross with the fingers that he had left.

Gabriel helped him up out of the seat, looked at the man's appearance, and figured he could walk. He assessed the amount of blood spread on the floor, knowing the majority of it was from his new acquaintance. He took a picture of the leader and sent it to his ex-handler in the CIA with a message saying, *"I'm out. Here is the last hit that I'll ever do for you."*

He looked at Raul's hands and ripped one of the dead men's shirts into strips and made a makeshift bandage out of it, wrapping his hands with enough clean material to protect them from bacteria as they made their way through the jungle. He let Raul put his weight on his shoulder and knew that he would never make it out of the jungle with this man in his current condition.

Gabriel took him back out towards the front and hid him in the corner. He ran across the courtyard to a soft-top jeep and turned it over, checking that it had gas. He moved to the other vehicles and crawled underneath them. They were giant transport trucks, and Gabriel used his knife to puncture the gas tanks. As the gas made its way down the driveway, he climbed into the jeep, pulled it around, and half-carried Raul into the backseat where he passed out almost instantly. The thought of relief and sanctuary was more than he could handle.

Gabriel sped past the cars, pulling a flare from his vest and tossing it beneath the vehicles lined up in the yard. The men running and screaming after them never saw it coming. The cars erupted across the yard one after another in a succession of fireballs, lighting the dark night, some of them flipping in the air. Gabriel shifted it into top gear, putting as much space as he could between himself and the compound. He didn't know if there would be anyone left to tell the story of what happened but hoped that everyone that had deserved it, lay dead.

The two men drove hard through the night, stopping

outside of Manuas where Gabriel called one of the company doctors, certain that he wouldn't know about his parting of ways with the CIA. He spoke quickly and explained the injuries. He had gone over the man, giving him a field check to see what if anything else seemed wrong with him. After seconds, he was sure that the man would need to have his ribs taped tightly and his hands disinfected and wrapped to protect what fingers were still left on each hand.

Two hours later, he had filled the jeep back up and thanked the doctor. The two men headed to the rendezvous point where they would abandon it and fly to safety and freedom. He promised Raul once they got to North America, it was going to be very difficult for them to get rid of him once he went up knocking on the front doors of Langley. He had information that no one else did, and that would be enough to give them good reason to keep him around.

Gabriel parked a few miles away from the landing strip. He pulled into a patch of trees, circling through the jungle until the jeep was lost in the brush. Raul asked, "How long until we are able to get out of here? They will find us eventually; there are eyes everywhere. You and I will die if they find us."

Gabriel pulled his satellite phone, hoping that it was the last call he would need to make on it. He looked over at Raul, shaking his head no, "I'm not that easy to kill. They paid a lot of money for me to learn what I can do and I do it very well."

Raul, having seen a short example of this, nodded thinking that maybe he *was* diabo branco, the *white devil*. The two men sat in silence as Gabriel contemplated the future, and Raul was praying that, by some chance, the two of them would make it out of there and live yet another day.

Just as he was readying himself to call, the light above them went dark. The two looked up and saw the Widow Maker flying high above them, shading everything for a moment with the cargo plane's wingspan. The plane circled around, coming in low in a field, and then coming to a stop. The rear of the plane opened and Gabriel floored the jeep back out of the jungle's edge and towards the plane.

Forsyth came out of the back of the plane, holding a machine gun to his shoulder already raised, aiming sharp at the two men. He lowered it when he saw Gabriel holding up one hand. He lowered the rifle for a moment, and then, to Gabriel's surprise, brought it back up quickly. Gabriel reached for his own gun, pulling it out to aim at Forsyth, hoping that he had not been double-crossed. He knew the CIA and wouldn't put it past them to try and take him out quickly. He peered into the rearview mirror of the jeep for a second and saw a small army of men coming out of the tree line.

Gabriel floored the jeep, yelling to Raul and pointing at the gas pedal. "Keep it down, and keep us on the path towards the plane. Gabriel climbed up out of his seat, standing with his machine gun, and took aim at the men closing in on the jeep.

Gabriel squeezed the trigger, taking the men out one after another. They rolled up next to the plane where Raul practically fell out of the jeep and hobbled into the rear of the plane. Gabriel pulled the jeep around so that it was pointing at the men, who were still in pursuit. He jammed the gas pedal down hard as the engine screamed in protest. He reached under the backside of the jeep, securing the last trick he had in his bag. Gabriel put the jeep in drive and got clear of the vehicle. It raced wildly across the field, bouncing and jumping. When it got within thirty yards of the pursuing men, Gabriel hit the switch, setting the blast from beneath the jeep. It flew over backwards, making the men veer their vehicles. Gabriel motioned to Forsyth to run inside and the two sprinted up the back entrance, punching the button to raise and close the back cargo door.

Once inside, Forsyth moved with purpose to the front of the long plane. He pushed the throttle levers up slowly at first and then quickly, making the men almost lose their balance. He was thankful as hell that he had left the plane running.

Raul hobbled to a seat and collapsed into it. With a bandaged hand, he made a sign of the cross, thanking God that someone out there was looking out for him. Gabriel walked to the front of the plane where Forsyth looked over, smiling. "Great to see you again, Gabriel; it's always a pleasure to see you. We always have such pleasant times, don't we? My only complaint is you're such a boring guy."

Gabriel nodded his head. "Yes, we have the best of times."

Forsyth dropped his smile as they accelerated down the makeshift runway for takeoff. "I was being sarcastic, Gabriel. You fucking owe me like you will probably never be able to imagine. But you know I'd do anything for you CIA boys, right?"

"Well, to tell you the truth I retired today. I will no longer be sent into places of death to kill those that are worse. Someone else can go in and take care of people like that. The reason they don't want to just drop a fucking bomb is that they are too damn scared of pissing off politicians or letting people know that America doesn't agree with how they are treating their citizens. No, they'd rather try and keep things looking civilized and be able to blame the killings on the people revolting against those that have done wrong."

"So, you looking for a job then?"

Gabriel sat back, closing his eyes for the first time in days. "No, I think that I'm going to take a little vacation first and then after that, yes, I might need to get a job or two lined up. I can assume that my credentials will be plenty enough to get me set up, right?"

Forsyth pulled a cigar and handed one to Gabriel. He lit a wood match and rolled the cigar until the end glowed. "You know you're going to need someone in the beginning to help you get going."

Gabriel nodded his head. "Yeah, I can see that being

necessary. You have time to do your flight duties and be a handler?"

Forsyth took a pull off of the cigar and said, "Well, I can assure you safe passage from one country to another because of my own particular skill set, which may enough for you to consider me. I know that I can sell the shit out of a highly trained ex-spook who has got more kills under his belt than the bird flu. I got to ask you one question, though."

Gabriel, who was near sleep, said, "What's that?"

"How the hell did you ever get into this line of work?"

Gabriel looked over and said, "I don't like those who hurt others."

He took off his weapons, setting them on the ground and pulled off his sweat-soaked fatigue jacket. He reclined his seat, thinking of his past and not wanting to thank Forsyth for the unpleasant dreams he was about to have.

Chapter 2
History

May 13, 2013

Jacob sat in the massive lecture hall. A bald instructor, who had the tone of James Earl Jones, stood before the class waving his fist around with conviction. He taught as if he was preaching to the group. Jacob had already read the textbook before enrolling in the class, but was fascinated with the different approaches that the author, who was the man standing before them, took. He also was required to take the class as part of his degree. He could have tested out, but did not want to only because of the compelling teachings of the man.

Jacob had his smart phone by his side and tried multiple times to watch the Chicago Marathon results as they were about to come in. He swore every time he hit the reload button to try and regain signal strength, but it only advised there was no service available. He envied his sister and mother for having the ability to be there today. Jacob rubbed at his leg; he'd had minor microscopic surgery a few months ago and was still healing. He would have been there cheering them on, sitting next to his father at the finish line, had it not been for the scheduled tests later this week.

Jacob's sister, Jane, was ranked to be in the top twenty finishers. He thought of his sister and how she was made for the sport. Jacob was six foot one and he felt like the runt of the family. He watched the clock on the wall, unable to focus on the lesson of the day. He knew that had he been smarter, he wouldn't have even wasted his time coming to the class today. There was a lesson going on in front of him, but his head was hundreds of miles away. When the clock struck 1 P.M., Professor Logan wrapped up his speech and dismissed the class. His professor smiled at him as he went past. "Mr. August, that paper was very impressive. If you keep thinking like that, people are going to start publishing your work. You need to put some serious thought into thinking about your future, about the path that you are going to take. You realize that being a teacher's assistant as a sophomore would be quite impressive on your resume, if and when you apply to medical school.

Jacob questioned, "Medical school?"

The teacher nodded, clasping his fingers together and resting them on his thighs. "You and I both know that you could help people; you are too damn smart to do anything else."

"I haven't decided that far into the future yet. I can tell you, though, that your book really opened my eyes when I read it last semester. It really puts things into perspective."

The professor could only shake his head, smiling yet somehow not surprised. "You do realize that the class is only on chapter ten, right? You put them all to shame, Jacob."

Jacob shrugged. "I can't put a good book down, sir; it

just kind of sticks when I read it. I'd like to talk more about that teaching assistant job sometime, but I need to go, sir. My mom and older sister are both runners today in Chicago. I think that my sister is going to place in the top ten this year, if not win the damn thing; she's amazing."

"Well, son, I don't think that she is the only one in your family that is amazing. I hope they do great today. That is quite an accomplishment to be had. It's too bad that you couldn't have made it there, but I think that you are doing the right thing. You're keeping your studies up, and even with the knee, you would have been tempted to try to compete, anyway. Although it probably wouldn't have killed you if you had taken a day off from studying. You do realize that you don't need to try and graduate in two years, right? I've heard a lot of kids nowadays use the whole four years to complete a bachelor's degree."

Jacob shrugged, smiling playfully. "Yeah, that's what my dad keeps telling me. Of course, then he thinks of the idea that I can get the degree early, and he'll have a hundred thousand dollars less in student loans. He gets the biggest smile on his face."

"Well, now I think that you're just full of shit. Between your own running and academics, your family has yet to see a dollar in student loans."

"Yeah, well I like that version of the story better. I really gotta get going, though. Have a good rest of your day, sir."

"Tell your mom and sister that I said congratulations to the both of them."

Jacob nodded his head, trying to not be rude rushing out the door, but when he walked outside he felt the bad vibe coming from everywhere around him. Students were rushing, looking worried, through the halls of the building. He walked out into the courtyard, where he finally was able to get reception on his phone. He knew before he got it to work, that somewhere, something was horribly wrong. Jacob walked, not paying attention to anyone. He felt like he was in a tunnel and everything on the outside of his phone was blurry to him.

"Jacob… Jacob, are you reading the news? Have you heard from your family? Oh my god, I hope that you're okay! Jesus, I hope that they're okay!"

Jacob looked up slowly and in a daze. "Huh? What? Oh hey, baby. I was just, um, looking at this report."

His girlfriend hugged him tightly. He sat down on the grass and looked around; the world was spinning. "I need to try calling them. Can you call my sister while I try calling my dad? He surely would have his phone on him today. He was going to snap a picture for me as they crossed the finish line. I was trying to check it the entire class period, hoping to see her results but no luck came from it."

She picked up her phone, but Jacob already had his ready. They began calling the numbers, to no avail. Eventually, he set the phone down, looked around, and realized he was in central Iowa and had no way of getting the information he needed. He felt like he was a million miles away. He had no one to contact; there were no news sites set up yet, no official numbers to call, and Jacob was on his way to losing his mind. He pushed up, angry and frustrated with his circumstances. He was not sure what he should do or who to be angry with. "I have to go. I can't just sit here and wait."

"Well, let me come with you; you shouldn't be alone right now."

"Jenny, if my family didn't make it, then I *am* alone. I'm twenty years old, and all the family I have would be gone. I'm getting on a plane and heading out there; I can't wait."

"Planes have been grounded in Chicago. The news said that as soon as the blasts went off, they shut down Chicago. You can't get in or out. You'd just be on standby at the Des Moines Airport and stuck there, and that isn't going to do you any good."

Jacob dropped back down to his knees. He bent his

head down, resting it on the grass and punching at the ground. "I... I don't know what to do. Fuck it! Tell me what to do and I'll do it; I just can't sit here not knowing what is happening there—I'll lose my god damn mind!"

Jenny rubbed his back, leaning in, putting her arm around him and kissing the top of his head. "Let's go back to your place. We can get your phone charged. Eventually, they are going to have the news in order and post the phone numbers that you need to call. They have the numbers of all who are racing, don't they?"

Jacob nodded his head. "Yeah, they do all have the numbers, but it's going to be near impossible for them to sort that out. The report said that they suspect terrorists."

"Do you really think that they were terrorists, Jacob?"

"People that kill others in mass numbers are the pure definition of a terrorist."

They walked back through the campus towards his fraternity house. Jenny was trying to console him, but he didn't want to be touched. The look of worry was turning into an anger that she had never seen before on his face. Jacob stared straight ahead, focused very much on the people in front of him. Every face he saw that was looking more worried than his own was making him furious. Finally, when Jenny could not stand the silence any longer, she gripped his hand tightly until he put some of that focus on her. "What is it, Jenny? I'm sorry but I'm trying to think."

"You aren't thinking. You look like you're going to rip someone's head off. I don't understand what you are so mad about, babe. You don't look worried... you look angry."

Jacob stared at her and for the first time realized that he was very much in control of his emotions. These feelings were the ones that he truly wanted to have without question. He said, "Jenny, you are aware that my family's whereabouts are unknown, I'm stuck hundreds of miles away, and I have no realistic hope of getting there. As you've already stated, there's no chance in getting a flight to Chicago ... there's nowhere to go from here."

Jacob climbed the steps to his room, opened the door, and let the two of them in. He walked over to the television, flipping it on and turning it immediately to the news channel. He didn't need to, as every one of the channels was already set to the disaster that was quickly becoming Jacob's entire existence, consuming him more by the second.

"Just have faith, Jacob. You still don't have any idea if they are all right or not. I mean, really, what are you thinking? You act like they're already dead. You have to have faith."

Jacob turned and looked to Jenny. "My only thought is if they are alive—if they are unharmed—why haven't they called? Can you honestly tell me there would be anything that could keep you from calling me, your dad, your mom, or your brother? Of course there isn't. Like I said, they must be gone. If they aren't, I will thank God himself and then kill them all for not calling my ass the very minute they got to safety."

The television constantly repeated information about the incident until it went black. A number came across the screen with a website address beneath. The message stated, *"For more information, please call the number below or visit the website. You can enter the number of the runner you need to inquire about. We are trying to get as many people in the database as we can."*

Jacob walked up to the television, raising his foot. Jenny screamed, "Jacob, stop! You need to relax—you need to start thinking. Christ, call the number, please. Let's find out what's going on and then we'll get it figured out. I'm here for you, but you have to want me to be here."

Jacob lowered his foot then he pulled up his laptop, unsure if he could handle dealing with any type of call. He focused for a moment, brought the computer to life, and punched at the keys, making sure to type them correctly. He reached the website that had been created that stated "Survivor's Database" on the main page. *Please enter the six-digit number of the runner about whom you are inquiring.* He typed in the number for his sister; after the sixth digit, he wavered his finger above the enter key, full of fear and hope at the exact same time.

He closed his eyes and hit enter. The report came back up, with a picture of her at the time of getting her race number. A simple message came up stating *Deceased. August, Jane age 24. Please contact 555-720-4552 to make arrangements. The city of Chicago and its citizens are very sorry for your loss from this tragic event. God bless you, and God bless America.*"

Jacob's fists were clenched next to the keyboard. He took a long, deep breath, thinking that maybe… just maybe he wasn't called because his parents were in a hospital emergency room too busy or unable to make the call. He thought maybe they didn't have identification on them. Every ounce that they were running with was going to feel much heavier by the end of the race, so they never carried unnecessary weight.

He checked his mom's number carefully, making sure that he was entering it right. The only hope he had left was that his parents were still alive. He hit enter, realizing that he had no number for his dad because he was a bystander, along with tens of thousands of others. He knew that he would be in the closest stand to the finish line because he had paid good money to ensure that he would have a seat there. He hit enter and was crushed, feeling things he had never before felt in his young life. The screen read *Deceased. August, Kristen age 42. Please contact 555-720-4552 to make arrangements. The city of Chicago and its citizens are very sorry for your loss from this tragic event. God bless you, and God bless America.*

Jenny came up, hugging him from behind. "Jacob, I am so, so sorry, baby. I can't imagine what you are feeling right now. What can I do? We need to figure out what we can do to find out about your dad."

Jacob collapsed on the couch. He was having serious issues dealing with what he was seeing. The news report showed direct, new footage of the finish line. He stared intently at the screen, pausing it and focusing on the bleachers. He pointed to his father, dressed in a shirt that had his sister and mother's names written on it. He smiled for a moment, looking at Jenny. "Jenny, there's Dad! There he is— he's okay!"

Jenny stared at the image then hit the pause button to resume the broadcast. The bleachers where Jacob's dad had been sitting would never look the same again; it was now just a mass of metal. Bodies were strewn across the street in every direction. A black, smoking image in front of them rolled up into the air. The footage showed people running for their lives, only to have an equally effective second bomb go off.

Jacob said, "I need to call these numbers. I'm going to have to figure this all out. Jenny you'd better go; I'm not going to be good for much, I don't think."

"You don't have to be 'good' for anything. I just need you, honey. I am here to help; you can't do this alone. It's too much for you to handle right now."

"Don't tell me what I can and can't handle! Don't try and psychoanalyze me, damn it. Not now!"

"I'm just saying that..."

Jacob stood and lifted her, not forcefully, but firmly, off the couch and walked her out of the room. "I just need some time, Jenny. We can meet up in a few days when I get this all figured out. I just have so much to do and I don't know where to start."

"Then why won't you let me stay? There's no reason for you to go through this alone."

Jacob stared with dark and determined eyes. "I know you're here for me, Jenny, and I appreciate it. I just can't put into words what I'm feeling, but I can tell you that I'm feeling anger more than hurt. If I lose it, well, it might be best if you don't have to be here to witness it." Jacob pulled her tight, giving her a hug and a long kiss—the last one he would ever give to the woman who was madly in love with him. Jenny let the tears begin to fall.

"I'll call you later, Jacob."

He nodded and closed the door slowly behind her, watching as she made her way down the hallway. As she passed Jacob's best friend, Brady, he saw the state that she was in and stepped in front of her. Brady towered over her as he placed his hands on her shoulders. "What happened? Are you all right, Jenny? Is it Jacob?"

She nodded as the tears grew heavier. He hugged her, and she said, "His family was at the marathon, you know. Well, they were there when... when..." She couldn't bring herself to say the words out loud.

Brady pushed her back, holding her at arm's length. "Wait, one of them was a victim? Who was it? His sister... or was it one of his parents?"

She wiped at her tears, unable to keep up with them. "No... all of them... he lost his entire family in one fucking blast. I don't know if he can handle this right now. I think he's losing it; he was scared to have me in the room. There were reports that it was terrorists, but they didn't have any information yet. They said they were reviewing the video footage."

Brady let go of her and leaned hard against the wall. "His entire family. Fuck. I need to go talk to him."

"I think he wants to be left alone. I mean, I really think he doesn't want to be bothered. I have never seen him this... this *angry*."

Brady tried to think of it from his perspective, and how he would feel if the tables were turned and it was his own family. He thought there was a strong chance he'd put a fist through every fucking wall in the house—or until he couldn't lift his arms any longer to cause more damage. He looked up with a few tears in his own eyes. "Don't worry about Jacob. I mean, I know you will, but trust me when I say that I will look out for him. I will stop in a little bit and check on him, all right? If he needs a few minutes to cool off, then that might not be a bad idea. I don't want to get pushy. He has every ability a man would need to be dangerous."

"Dangerous?"

"Yeah, I play football; Jacob breaks boards and bricks. I think I'll give him a bit to relax, then I'll stop in to see him soon, okay? Just go ahead and head home. I'm sure that he will give you a call later. If not, I'll text you. Just give him some space; he might need it."

She thought about Jacob and realized that if he was upset and couldn't control himself, it might be best for him to be alone. She had seen him compete in many competitions and had seen, firsthand, the pain he could instill in others when need be. "Just make sure that you check on him. You let me know how he's doing. He really needs someone right now... I just don't think he knows it yet."

Brady nodded. "He's my boy. Don't worry; I'll take care of him. Go on home or back to class, whatever you got going on. We'll make sure he stays on the right path."

She leaned in, gave him a hug, and kissed his cheek. "You're an angel, Brady. Thank you so much. I really appreciate it."

*****

Brady walked up to the door and knocked. When Jacob opened the door, Brady tried to not look surprised at his appearance. His eyes were bloodshot and he didn't look like his normal self. Brady couldn't blame him for it, but at the same time, he was used to seeing him steady as a rock—the kind that never broke. He was the toughest man that Brady knew.

He gave a half-assed smile and held up a bag. "I got sandwiches for you. I thought you might want some supper. How are you holding up?"

Jacob said, "I'm not hungry and I'd rather be alone."

Brady moved in past him, putting the food and drinks down on the coffee table. "Sorry man, but you don't know what you need right now. Come eat something. Hey, have you been watching the news this whole time?"

Jacob nodded. "Yeah, I am having a fucking hell of a time trying to wrap my head around it. The reports said that they have the fuckers who did it pinned down in some apartment. I wish I was there with them right now."

"Yeah, it'd be nice to see them being brought to justice once they finally give up."

"Fuck bringing them to justice. I don't want to see them serve a minute of time!"

"What are you talking about, man? How the hell can you feel that way?"

"Because I would kill them. I'd slit the throats of every single one of them and let them bleed to death in front of me. Do you know what the wounded count was? There were hundreds of people injured. I mean, really, it's actually a miracle more people didn't die. But I don't think they deserve to live; they hurt so many families and forever altered too many lives."

Brady sat down and stared at his friend. He was filled with anger and conviction, and Brady believed every single word that came out of his mouth. Jacob was not talking just to talk; he knew his friend better than that. He was confident that if he got the opportunity, he would take full advantage of it. "Do you actually think you could … you could go through with something like that?"

Jacob didn't answer; he just nodded his head ever so slightly, staring coldly at the television, which had the suspects' pictures on it. Any questions that Brady had about his friend being able to do such a thing had been laid to rest.

Jacob looked at the food, and when his stomach growled, he decided he should eat. The two sat down and dined on sandwiches. Brady asked, "Hey, have you called Jenny... you know, to let her know that you are doing okay? She was worried sick about you earlier. I think if you just sent her a text letting her know you're okay, she'd feel much better. It would only take you a second to knock out."

Jacob sat back and typed out a quick message, letting her know he was all right, but that he was going to stay in for the night and get a hold of those he needed to, to make arrangements. He would probably be on the phone the rest of the night and not have a chance to call. After arranging for his family to come back to town, he would have to find a funeral home and get in touch with the family lawyer. Jacob's head was spinning trying to think of everything he had to do. It was on all his shoulders because there was no one else to do it. He thought of all the crying faces on the news and tried to figure out when he would have the time to grieve. *How long would it take before he felt normal again?*

Jacob finished his sandwich, slapped Brady on the back, and stood up. He made his way to the door and slid out without saying anything else. As he walked through the university's courtyard, he saw one of his professors sitting on a bench by himself. He tried not to make eye contact, but the professor had seen him. "Mr. August, do you have a minute that we can speak?"

Jacob looked up and waved, giving a smile that didn't hold much conviction. "Hey, uh, Dr. Logan, how goes it?"

Logan patted the empty wooden bench next to him, motioning for him to come and take a seat. "Can you join me for a minute, son? I'd like to have a talk with you, please."

Jacob shook his head. "Sorry, sir, I don't think I can talk right now. I'm not in that good of a place."

"Sit down, Mr. August. I've already spoken with Jenny and she thinks that you need to speak to someone."

"Don't worry, sir, I'll be all right. I just need to get some stuff off my shoulders."

"No... no, you won't. I don't know if you ever will. Are you aware that you have a disorder?"

"Sir, I don't think I'm in the mood to be able to handle anything that isn't an absolute necessity right now. I really do appreciate the fact that she contacted you. It was very sweet of her. But you see, I have too much to—"

Logan cut him off. "Sit down, August, and shut up; we need to talk. I'm sorry to be so blunt, but I feel you aren't going to listen to me any other way. Sit now... please."

Jacob sat down, looked closely at the man, and nodded that he was ready to listen. The professor had never been so rash with him before. Logan pulled out a pack of cigarettes, staring into the distance. "Jacob, don't take this wrong, because what I'm going to tell you is not a bad thing whatsoever. Do you know what I did before I was a teacher Jacob?"

Jacob felt like his day couldn't get much worse and thought he might as well sit in for the long haul. "I just thought you were probably a psychologist of some type with a private profession. You wrote a book and then you went on to get offered a teaching position, which you were kind enough to humbly accept."

Professor Logan smiled. "Well, just about everything after the book is accurate. I think what's important here is that you know I was not a psychologist in the standard terms... you know, in private practice, helping children with mommy and daddy issues, or a wife that is upset with a cheating husband and trying to deal with it emotionally."

"So, what kind of consultations did you do?"

"I helped killers, Jacob. I helped them deal with their emotions."

"What do you mean 'killers'? Were you in a prison?"

"What I say now stays between us, whether you accept or decline what I have to ask. Is that understood, Mr. August?"

Jacob nodded slowly. "You are kind of creeping me out, sir."

Logan tapped his cigarette on a zippo and lit it, knowing this was always a delicate part of the recruitment process. "I helped killers; men who did it for a living. You see, son, I worked with the CIA. They have men who use a special skill set because they've trained them to do that. What I did was deal with the aftermath of these men."

"Aftermath?"

"We send these men to school. We teach them how to kill as effectively and efficiently as we can. The problem is, you can train someone to be a master killer, but if someone can't mentally handle it, they aren't going to have much longevity in the business. Killing is an art, and it's not particularly pretty. Things don't always happen as we want them to; at that point, we need to be able to help them deal with it. If not, they can go through some—excuse my French—some fucking scary times. Some of those jobs will come back and haunt them. If you they aren't wired to deal with it, they usually end up eating a bullet themselves. Or they break out of the CIA mold and go on a crusade, killing anyone based on their own rules and their own brand of justice."

"So, you helped men deal with killing people? How did you get into that… and why the fuck are you telling me all this? Especially on a day like today. I've got enough shit going on right now."

"You have the type of personality that they look for. You see, I still send a few applicants their way. I have an eye for people. Sometimes I see a student that can read people like nobody's business. I send them off to interview and see about being a profiler for the FBI or CIA."

"And the others?"

"Well, sometimes I see a young man, if I could take you for example; you won't be offended, will you?"

Jacob shook his head, letting Logan continue. "Well, I look at you; you are highly intelligent—we both know that. I know you are in activities, but you seem less worried about them than those around you. You work hard and you are withdrawn from others. You don't seem to want to put yourself out there for people in the sense of relationships. You only care about your family, and now you don't even have that. You have something deeper eating at you now, something that you aren't sure exactly how to release. Something that might turn your insides black over time."

"So, you think that I could be the...?"

"With your mind and your ability to not get emotionally involved, I think there is no limit to your potential, Jacob. The fact that you are at genius-level intelligence and have the physical prowess that is needed for the job, only makes you that much more perfect to work for the company."

Jacob stood up and stared at him, waiting for him to smile and confess that he was only fucking with him. "You are kidding, right? You're pulling my leg and you wanted to mess with me? You think that maybe making me laugh might help somehow, and you picked some sick and twisted way to do it?"

"Jacob this is serious. I've been retired from the CIA for ten years, but I find men who can perform certain necessary functions in the world that others can't... that others don't want to know about. You would be well compensated. I know that you probably like the thought of murdering the men that did this to your family. You probably can't get the thought of that very act out of your mind, can you?"

Jacob nodded and just barely whispered it. "I'd like to murder them all. I'd like to slit their throats and hurt them in the worst ways that I can imagine."

"How do you think you would handle that if they put you in a room with... let's say a knife, and you had the opportunity and a green flag to take the men out? What if something like that could be arranged, Jacob?"

Jacob stared intently, no humor on his face whatsoever. "Can it be arranged?"

Logan nodded his head. "I can't this time. This is too high profile of a case right now. If they aren't shot dead by the officers, there are going to be people screaming from the hill that they need to be brought to trial. They need to be brought to justice, and there will be no way to get around that. They will turn into heroes in the eyes of those who think the same way they do. If that happens, the backlash that America could see and feel because of it will be detrimental. This will not be the last time. Time has proven that this will happen again. But if we have men and women who can take out the threats before they hit, then we stand a chance. We stand a good chance, but we need people now." He stared at Jacob, thinking for a moment. "We need men like you; people who won't lose sleep, who won't lose their mind when the time comes to work."

Jacob sat back and ran his hands through his hair, contemplating the path that had been suggested against the goals his parents had for him. He thought about his own goals that he wanted to conquer. Before today, he never would have considered a path that might lead to him being a killer for hire. He thought of Jenny, the men who set the bombs, his sister, and his parents. He thought of the funeral that he, alone, would be in charge of overseeing. "Who do I talk to?"

Logan tapped his smoke, knocking ashes off of its end. He pulled a card from his pocket and handed it over to him. "Here, you call this man. His name is Tony Baker; I've already spoken to him about you, and he's expecting your call. He's already working out the details, but he knows you will probably be busy for the next few weeks."

"So, I just call this number… and then what?"

"You go to school, much like now, except they teach you a skill set you will not get anywhere else. If you can keep your head on your shoulders after a job, which is harder than pulling a trigger, then you'll be all right. The blood is easier to wipe from your hands than your soul, of course."

Jacob hammered the nail in the coffin, erasing any doubts that Logan may have had about him when he asked, "You think there is something about killing a monster that would make me feel bad for them? Something that would keep me from doing it? There is nothing that would stop me; nothing that would make me feel remorse for those pieces of shit."

"It's easier to say that than to actually do it. But I think you have that special quality they need. Do you want me to send Tony a message and advise him that there is a chance you're going to do it? You think this is something you could be capable of handling?"

Jacob tapped the card a few times with his finger, staring at it. He realized his stars would never be lined up quite like they were at that moment; this was the time to act on them. He slid it in his pocket, nodding his head. "Please tell him to expect a call from me. I need to get my family settled and then I'll contact him. School will be out for the summer and it would be nice if I could start then."

"Maybe you don't understand something about it. There are no summer breaks, Jacob. Once you go into this, it's your life until you see fit to retire. If you end up being that good, they have been known to have the experienced hitters train the younger men who need some final guidance."

"Can I marry or have children?"

"Yes, of course you can. You couldn't tell them what you really do for a living, but someone with your personality isn't going to want to worry about children or a wife. You aren't wired for it, son."

Jacob walked back and forth for a moment, contemplating even further. "Well, I guess maybe I should just take a night to think on it; maybe take a couple?"

"Take as long as you need. But if that feeling you have now is still there in a week, there's a very good chance that you'll be making the right decision, son. You could be one of the best—you just need to try. I think whatever you do, you will be something special. I just don't see the point of you missing an opportunity that can help shape and change the world, as we know it. You can save the pain of millions because of a single action. How many people do you know can say that, son? I will tell you; it is a very limited number."

Logan held out his hand and Jacob looked at it for a second before shaking it. Logan said, "I truly am sorry about your loss and want to give you, and any family you have left, my sincerest words that things will get better. You will move on and make your family proud. If you need anything at all, son, call me directly. I have my number on the back of that card. Please don't hesitate to call me day or night.

Jacob firmly shook his hand, nodding his head. "Thank you very much, Professor Logan. I really appreciate it. I have a feeling this is going to be good for me. It may cause pain, but it will be to those who deserve it. I'll call your friend after I have a little time to look at my options. My dad always said to not go about rushing into shit, or you'll find yourself neck deep in it."

Logan smiled. "Well, it would seem your father is... excuse me, was a smart man."

Jacob smiled briefly. "Yeah, I'm glad, regardless of whether he's here or in heaven, that I am able to call him my dad. He was great… always will be, and I'll hold close all the memories of him and the rest of my family."

"I'm sure you will. Now go and do what decision making you need to so you can move forward with your life one way or another."

Jacob gave him a short salute and headed back to his fraternity house where he didn't sleep a wink; instead, he wrote down pros and cons and did research on the internet. The only moment's peace he got was when he found out that one of the men responsible for the Chicago attack had been killed and the other shot and in critical condition.

He lay in bed with his hands behind his head, imagining himself walking into the hospital, no one the wiser as to who he was, making his way up through the service entrance, slipping past a guard, and putting something in the man's IV bag. It would be very painful and slow acting, but eventually fatal. He smiled, thinking of radiation poisoning, making him suffer for weeks. He leaned over the side of his bed and fumbled with his pants, looking for the card that Professor Logan had given him. He smiled again, thinking of the opportunities that might present themselves.

He pulled it from his pocket and read the simple card. He thought of Jenny and how he would tell her that he had signed up for a job that would require him to leave for a good while. Hell, he wasn't even sure if he would be able to let her know that he had signed with the CIA. He was worried she would judge him. She was there for the long haul, while he was distant and unsure of what he wanted for himself long term. As much as he loved her, he didn't see the relationship lasting until the end.

Jacob pulled out his phone to make two of the most difficult calls of his life. He dialed Jenny, who answered with a sleepy yawn. "Hey, Jenny it's me. I, uh, think that we should talk."

Jenny, who was not fully awake yet asked, "Hey, baby, did you get a chance to talk with Professor Logan? I was hoping that he might help you feel a little better since I was doing such a bad job. I wasn't sure if Brady was going to be able to help you much, either.

Jacob sat for a moment, unsure what to tell her. "Brady brought me some food and told me that you asked him to come check on me. So, thank you; I definitely needed to eat. I didn't stay long with him though. I had been in that room all day and I needed to get out of there and stretch my legs, if you know what I mean. I did run into Logan while I was out. He actually had some interesting information for me about a job he thought I might want to try and apply for. He gave me a card for one of the company's recruiters, but told me that it was probably a good idea if I put some consideration and thought into it."

Jacob could tell that Jenny was much more awake at the mention of jobs and job offers. She was a sophomore as well and was well aware that offers weren't rolling into students; especially students who still had years left of college. It was hard enough, she knew, to get your foot in the door with help and a bachelor's degree. She was puzzled at what he was talking about, although she knew how intelligent and gifted he was. "Well, is a job offer something that you are interested in right now? I mean, a lot just happened. A lot more is going to change. You know what I mean, baby? I just want to make sure it isn't something you are going to jump into just to regret later in life. I'd hate to have you throw away a scholarship just to try something you aren't sure about."

"I'm just considering it, but it would mean me having to move, most likely, and then I assume I would be assigned somewhere else at some point."

He wasn't actually assuming; he knew damn well that they picked where he went, what he ate, and what he wore if they wanted to. He knew that most likely they'd start him out with some bullshit diplomatic position so that he could be overseas. Then at some point, they would give him a real assignment and that would be his life going forward.

"So, you still haven't totally made up your mind. I mean, there is time for the two of us to talk about... you know... *us*. I really like you, Jacob." She laughed a little. "Well, I don't like you, but I love you with all my heart. I think that we have something together. I know that you have your issues with being close to people, but I really think we can work through them. I mean, I'm in it through thick and thin if you think you can handle it, baby."

"Can we talk tomorrow some more? I just wanted to call and let you know that I appreciated you looking out for me. I probably wouldn't have done as well today if you hadn't been around to keep me calm and my head on straight."

"I love you, honey. Promise me you will try and get some sleep tonight. You don't need to stay up trying to figure everything out, okay? You can't solve the world's problems in one day, right babe?"

Jacob laughed, already seeing himself punching the numbers to call Tony Baker to tell him he wanted to get an interview set up for as soon as his family had been laid to rest. "Yeah, you know, I'm thinking about getting to bed here soon. Let's try to talk tomorrow. We'll have to see what's going on first; I don't know everything yet."

He hung up the phone, tapped in the number, and hit send. After two rings, a deep voice answered. "Hello, thank you for calling, Mr. August."

"Hi... wait, how the hell did you know...?"

"Christ, son, if I can't figure out something like caller ID then I need to get a new profession. Logan said you're smart. Well, not smart, he said you're a downright genius and that you would be the kid for the job. We have a whole shit ton of tests that we're going to run you through, up one side and down the other. In the end, if they come back and tell us that you would be best suited shooting people in the head or slitting their throats, we'll sign you up the next day."

"What do I do, Mr. Baker?"

"You take care of your family. You finish school this semester and you come down to Virginia in a month and you get tested and accepted."

"So, it's a sure thing?"

"You got past Professor Logan's radar and that is plenty good enough for all of us here at Langley. We have a need for men like you. There aren't many out there that can be recycled time and time again. One day we'll run out, I'm sure of it. So, we take care of all those pieces of shits that we can now. How does that sound to you, son?"

"I'm finding this a little too easy, to tell you the truth. Shouldn't this be a little more complicated?"

"It usually is, son. Hell it usually is a big damn pain in the ass. There is one reason that you can walk the red carpet, kid—we need you."

Jacob who was more than a little curious said, "Yeah, I

think I'm getting more questions the longer you speak."

"We can put you to work almost immediately. We think your backstory will be better if you finish school this year, but at the exact same time, I think that you have demons in you that you are ready to put to rest. The quicker you start doing it, the better it is for you. I do have one sad fact for you, son. You want to hear it?"

"Sure."

"You're going to receive the best mental and physical training in the world. The problem for you, the thing that is going to drive you insane with rage and anger, is the realization that you won't learn this overnight. It won't be that easy; you'll have to trust your instructors and take your time. Because if someone thinks they can rush through the training process, they'll be the ones lying out on a slab before they know it. The enemy is scared of the CIA. We do the dirty work, and the world knows it. But the problem is, if you make a mistake, they will shoot you dead without hesitation—none whatsoever. Is that something you think you can handle? If I promise you—and I do promise you, Jacob— that we can help you take those things out, that we can help you rid yourself of some of that pain you have pent up, can you be patient enough to wait for it?"

"If it means that I can help people and that I'll live another day then, yes, I think I can wait. I just want to start as soon as possible. I'm not really worried about school. Professor Logan laid it out pretty well earlier tonight for me. He mentioned that if we start this path, if I take this lesser-traveled road, there will be no turning back. There will be nothing but full steam ahead and I won't have to worry about another day in class. He told me I'd still be in school, but it would be an entirely different game. It would be something that would give me the skills and assets, as long as I am patient."

"Logan is a smart son of a bitch. My god, if he would have had the ability to forget the things he'd done, he would have been one scary son of a bitch."

"Well, he did say that not everyone is able to handle the job. He made it pretty clear that he thought I could, Mr. Baker."

"You wouldn't be on the phone with me if he didn't think so. I am glad that you gave me a call tonight. It's nice to know that there are still people out there to help us deal with the troubles that need put away. Give me a call in a week, kid. If you don't give a shit about finishing classes, well it sure as hell isn't going to bother us if you skip out. We can put you up for a while until the next session starts. There is plenty of information you can study in the meantime. We'll be able to keep you plenty busy; there are plenty of files you could work on with having that psych background."

"But I want to work in the field. I don't want to end up being an office grunt, sir."

"Hey! Those office grunts are important; I promise you that. Their intel will keep you alive one day. But I do guarantee we aren't trying to pull you in just to make you do some job that you hate. We are pulling you in out of nowhere for one reason, and one reason only—we want to have you take out the people that don't belong here. God knows there are plenty of them, and we think you'll be a great fit at the company, kid. Try and keep where you're going on the down low and don't tell anyone that doesn't need to know."

"What about my best friend and my girlfriend?"

"Let me ask you this, because if you haven't thought about it, you should. Is she still going to be your girlfriend, is she going to be okay with you leaving for six months without any phone calls or emails?"

"I think she… well, I know that she loves me, sir, but I don't know if she could handle me living a lifestyle like we are talking about."

"Then she isn't the one for you; she won't be able to know, anyway. All anyone needs to know about you is that you're a diplomatic assistant until the day you retire—or depending on your health. Sometimes we just bring you back to Langley, where you get to teach future spooks how to be the most effective killers they can be. But that shouldn't be until you hit forty-five or fifty years old. If you can't lie to those you love, then there is a good chance you shouldn't be trying to date that person. A lot of our men are loners. There isn't anything wrong with that. It can get lonely, but the job is what keeps them moving and working."

Jacob opened his mouth to speak, realizing the truth of what he was saying was difficult. "I think that I understand. We will be in touch soon, sir. Thank you for your time."

"You as well, Jacob. My deepest condolences regarding your family."

****

The following week was the most depressing week of Jacob's life. But it was also one of the most highly anticipated. He had to think about the unknown, imagining what the job would be like and trying to think of what the downsides would be. He had to also meet his family at the Des Moines International Airport. The funeral director met him there with a van to pick up his sister and parents. He followed them to the funeral home where he gave the director the dresses that his mother and sister regularly wore to church and a black suit for his father.

On the day of the funeral, the priest spoke of things that Jacob could not have disagreed more with, if he tried. He knew that loss was inevitable and that death and taxes were the only things guaranteed in life. He smiled when the priest said that everything happens for a reason. The only reason Jacob could see was that, in God's eyes, he had chosen him to cure the world of those that had wronged it. He thought of the angel of death named Gabriel, a holy warrior, and thought that if he was allowed to choose his field name, it would be most appropriate.

Jacob looked behind him, seeing family members that felt they should be here to help support him. They could only say how nice everyone was, how great it was to get to see everyone, and how it was such a tragedy. He also noticed that very few of them were able to offer a personal story to him. Jacob could only stand in the corner, out of the way, staring blankly, not sure what to say to people. He found it odd that as people grew in age, they only came together for birth and death; he was damn sure that there was no birth to be celebrated here today.

Chapter 3
Small Pleasures

September 21, 2024 1:00 A.M.

Billionaire software developer and newly widowed Steven Riddick made his way through the party. He had a bottle of champagne in one hand and a cigarette in the other, held between two skinny fingers. The crowd stared at the man with sad eyes. They could not imagine what losing an entire family in one fleeting moment could or would feel like. Wives, who were also mothers, reached their hands out to console him and whisper sweet words of kindness and faith. They were impressed that he was even trying to fulfill his social obligations. Steven nodded his head, a very relaxed look on his face. The bottle in his hand had not been the first of the night. Whispers from businessmen to their wives and girlfriends about how the company would fail. He would not be able to handle the loss of his family and still be able to run a Fortune 500 company.

Steven walked out of the party's reserved room and made his way to the coat check. He set the bottle of champagne on the counter and fished in his pocket for the retrieval ticket. A young, slim, and plentiful brunette stared at him. She knew exactly who Steven was. She collected his ticket, disappeared into the countless racks of clothes, and brought out a light fall jacket. She said, "Make sure and wear this Mr. Riddick. You don't want to get a cold."

Riddick looked up for the first time, seeing a generous pair of breasts and not much else. He fumbled with his words, saying drunkenly, "Oh, it's not even close to being too cold, dear. There's still at least another month of driving with my top down."

"Wow, you must really like the fresh air on your face, huh, Mr. Riddick?"

Riddick leaned in on his elbows, blowing a plume of smoke to the side and smiling. "Well, I like many things with their tops down."

The woman, who was a good thirty years younger than Steven, smiled. She knew that he had lost his wife and family in a horrible accident recently. She wasn't sure if he was drunk, desperate, or just a complete asshole. "Sir, are you okay to drive home tonight? You seem to have had a little too much to drink."

"Why, dear? Are you offering to give me a ride? Because I would love a ride from you." He peered at the small metal pin on her shirt and went back to eye contact. "Julie."

She smiled, but was very uncomfortable about the conversation. "Sir, would you like me to call a driver service or arrange for you to be able to stay at the hotel this evening? I don't want anything happening to you because you drank and drove."

Riddick, seeing that the ride from Julie wasn't going to happen, stubbed out his smoke and reached for another immediately. He bid her a drunken salute, smiled with a shrug, and stumbled down the hallway to the valet to pick up his sports car. When he saw the news reporters outside the building, he sobered up for a moment, stubbing out the newly lit cigarette and putting the bottle under his coat.

He walked out with his shoulders high and a practiced look of sadness on his face and gave the valet his card. News reporters and paparazzi screamed for him. He'd been in seclusion for the last month since laying his family to rest. He raised a hand, smiling. "I'm sorry, but I'm just not ready to talk yet. If this hadn't been my best friend's fundraiser for children's cancer research, I would be at home this evening. I appreciate all of the kind words in the media lately. Don't worry, Riddick Software and Development will not falter. It will remain the leader in its field; I promise you!"

The valet came up and opened the door for Riddick, who fell into the seat and set the bottle and jacket upright carefully, so as not to spill it in front of the nation's largest news media outlets. He also didn't want to spill the champagne on the Italian leather seats that he loved so much. He held up a crisp hundred-dollar bill for the valet who eagerly snatched it, a smile in his eyes. Riddick waved to the crowd and punched the gas, speeding down the streets of Chicago.

****

An hour later, the much drunker Riddick, who was feeling every bit of his fifty-eight years, drove up the long, winding driveway on the outskirts of Chicago. The private entrance to his country estate was secluded. Mature oak trees created a green canopy enclosure above him. The top was down on his Mercedes SL63 and a cool, crisp breeze blew through his aging light hair. A bottle of champagne lay empty in the seat next to him. He pulled up to his house, leaving the car's top down. He knew the thieves of the city weren't an issue this far out of town.

Steven Riddick paid a lot of money to be able to sleep well at night. He studied the front of his house and why it was so dark. Every light was off in the twenty-room house. Its shadows gave him the creeps; they looked evil. He had never wanted this house. His late wife had made him buy the estate. He would've been much happier in a condo in the city. Right now, the moon was the only source of light. He checked his Rolex and saw that it was almost one in the morning.

He got out and immediately realized he was much

more inebriated than he thought. He fell against the car door and gripped it with both hands to keep from losing his balance. He wasn't "falling down" drunk yet, but he knew from experience that he was close, and he was confident he could get there with another bottle of bubbly.

He straightened out his blue suit and made a drunken stagger up the steps, tripping and cursing the decision to drink as much as he had. Steven's new goal was to make it to his king-size bed where he would have no issues with falling asleep. Steven laughed, thinking of his fall on the large stone steps. He could just picture the headlines: "Billionaire Found Dead on Front Steps: Cracked-Open Head Likely the Cause".

He made it to the front door, reaching for his keys while resting a forearm against the frame for balance. When Steven twisted the handle of the door, it opened without a key's assistance. Steven crashed through the door, curious as to what was going on in the brick palace. He slammed shut the large double oak doors, not caring about waking the staff. He threw his car keys on a side counter. The house was eerily quiet; there were no servants, no guards—nothing. It was the purest of silence. He passed off his worries that it was closer to breakfast than midnight at this point. "What the hell do I pay all you god damn people for if no one is ever here? I should fire every damn one of you. You're all useless."

He stumbled through the dark, searching for a light switch, which seemed impossible to find in his drunkenness. He made it about three steps into the hallway when he tripped over something out of place in the middle of the floor. He tried to right his balance, but it was too late and he was too damn drunk. He landed hard on his chest, smashing his face on the marble path. He screamed in pain and rage, "Oh my god, my nose! I broke my fucking nose! You're fired—every last one of you, god damn it!"

Steven reached for his nose to inspect the damage, expecting blood, but when he lifted his hands off the floor, they were already wet and sticky. He sniffed at it realizing his nose was worthless but still unsure what it was. He rolled on to his back, more than perturbed that he could feel wetness and stickiness through his shirt. It was the same foreign substance as on his palms. He brought out his phone, trying to swipe at it to get the light to come on. He finally succeeded; a light-blue light emitted from it, and the space in front of him lit up.

He pushed himself upright and focused the light on his body. It was hard to tell where the wetness and his dark blue suit began. He put his left hand out in front of him and put the light on it. His fingers became visible, and it looked like his hand was painted red. "What the fuck has been going on here?"

He aimed the light on the floor; when he saw what was in front of him, he muffled a scream, pushed backwards, and dropped the phone. He clumsily picked it back up and held it. The white floor, from his feet to the dark figure in front of him, was almost black with drying blood. His hand trembled, making it difficult to hold the phone steady.

He crawled up slowly until his light was strong enough to show him what was there. His bodyguard William, who he'd seen take on three men at one time and putting all of them in the hospital, lay flat and lifeless on the floor. Steven shook the man whispering, "William, William, what the hell is going on?"

When he didn't respond, Steven placed his fingertips under the man's thick, muscular neck, trying to feel for a pulse. There was nothing there. Steven gasped and stood up, slipping in the blood and landing back on his ass.

He dialed 911, leaving bloody fingerprints on the screen of the phone. He anxiously hit the send button but nothing happened; there was no connection. He stared at the phone in awe. There was no more expensive phone or plan that someone could have; a personal guarantee that was worthless at the moment. They swore they'd never leave you without service because service was exactly what you paid for.

The sound of dress shoes echoed on the imported Italian marble floor. They got louder as they got closer, filling the large, open entry space of the home. Steven stammered, "Who... who's there, what do you want?" No answer. "I said who is there? This is a private residence. I will have you know that the police are on their way here right now. I hope you can comprehend that. I just dialed 911 and they'll be here in no time. I have guards and they will stop you."

The man entered the room, giving off only a long shadow. "You do realize that dialing 911 and speaking to 911 are two very different things, Mr. Riddick. Your guards, which is really just 'a guard' is lying in front of you. I don't think there is going to be very much that he can do right now."

Steven was predictable in every way imaginable. Unfortunately for him, he didn't live in the same world of reality as normal people did. His mind had been brainwashed over the years with "yes men" walking behind him, telling him how he could never be wrong. He had been a rich man for too long, not knowing the limitations of a normal human. Riddick was relentless in his plea, though. "I... I have money. I can give you whatever you want. I can get you whatever you want."

The man in the dark continued his approach, slowly taking his time and staying just out of the light from the phone. A foot came from the shadows, connecting with Steven's hand and sending the thin, sleek phone into the air. The light from it caught the intruder's face for a moment; it was square and had the beginnings of a beard. The phone spun on the floor in a circle, the shadows dancing on the walls wildly until it came to a stop, and its glow faded as it went to sleep. "There's nothing you can do for me; it's men like you that keep me from sleeping at night."

"Men like me... men like me made this country what it is! What the hell did I do to you?"

The man stepped from the shadows, the moonlight barely exposing his face through the large windows that led up the double staircase. "My name is Gabriel. Your bodyguard, the one on the floor, whose throat is slit, tried to hire me for a job. I have been out of town, or this would have happened much sooner. But If I hadn't left at all then your family would be here as well."

"What job? What are you talking about? Please, I'm still grieving over the loss of my family. Just leave."

Gabriel screamed, "Do you think this a good time to lie? He tried to hire me to kill your family. To make it look like an accident. I'm sure he got my name from someone that was very important; it would seem they didn't mention it, or your man was too stupid to listen to my rules about who can and who can't die."

This shut the man up. He still didn't understand Gabriel's motives. He said, "I can pay you what you would have made. Money is no issue."

"Money is always the issue. Unfortunately, Mr. Riddick, you cannot buy your way out of this. I am doing this for free… of course, your software rivals will not be broken hearted."

"Well, for god sakes if you don't want money then why are you here?"

"You killed your entire family, that's why I—."

The man did not let him finish his sentence; he knew his time was short. "I didn't do anything to them. It was the bodyguard; I didn't know."

Gabriel, infuriated, took one step towards Steven and kicked him in the soft part of his stomach, sending him down flat on his back and knocking the wind out of him. When Steven tried to sit back up and catch his breath, Gabriel whipped him across the face with the butt of the gun. Fresh blood poured from the man's mouth. "You might not have pulled the trigger yourself, but you hired it out; that is good enough for me."

Steven in a last attempt, with blood and tears pouring down his face, pleaded to Gabriel, "I can do anything—I can change. Please, what is there that I can do for you? I want to live."

Gabriel took a step back staring at the man; blood and snot flowed freely at this point. As he lifted the pistol, the moon glimmered off the blued barrel. He pulled the hammer back. "You can pray that God has more compassion and mercy than I do."

He pulled the trigger once, sending a round through the front of the man's forehead. He collapsed back to the ground, hitting hard. Gabriel looked around seeing no one but the dead. He walked a can of gasoline around the room, spreading it everywhere. He lit a Zippo and dropped it on the floor, into a pool of gas.

The fire grew as it spread across the room and climbed its way up the walls and curtains. Gabriel smiled, knowing he played his part in helping to keep the balance between good and evil. When he went out the back, he left a folder documenting the man's actions.

Chapter 4
Other Hitters

September 13, 2024 9:00 P.M.

Harry walked up the long set of steps. He stopped when he saw that the light was out above his door. He looked behind him, making sure that no one was trying to follow him. Paranoia was a part of the trade, and one he thought he was particularly good at. He reached up with a hand, wiggling the light bulb. As soon as he touched it, he realized it had not simply burned out. He let go, pulled his pistol, and jumped into the air and out of the way. He landed hard and hit the flashlight attached to the pistol; he aimed it up the stairway, ready to fire. What he saw was an empty, wooden staircase leading up to the fourth floor. He smiled, thinking that a stupid coincidence and his paranoia might just be what kills him.

He pushed up off the ground and looked down the hall, hoping no one had seen him pull his gun out in public. Harry knew people would get a little skittish if he was pulling out guns in the middle of the apartment complex for no reason. He also knew it would be a little hard for people to believe he was a tax accountant if they saw that. He put the gun back in the holster. Harry walked to the condo's door for a second time, twisting the light bulb until it began shining. He opened the door and turned on the lights, tossing his coat and bag on the floor.

He thought about the damn light bulb again and played it off. Some teenager in the building was probably screwing with him. Harry hated kids for this very reason. He shut the door, and as he turned, he saw a pair of black wingtip shoes and dress slacks. He looked up and reached for his pistol; before he had a chance to pull it, an intense pain exploded in the back of his neck and everything went black. The last thing he remembered as he lay twitching on the ground was the wet, warm feeling of his own urine as it made its way down the front and sides of his pants.

Harry woke to a warm sting on his face followed by another one. He felt pressure from the top of his head and finally snapped out of his slumber. He realized it was not a warm sting. It was a phone book, slapping him across the face, and doing it hard and fast.

Harry blinked away tears, shaking his head. He moved his tongue through his mouth and spat. If it were his first time at the rodeo, he'd have been more curious about the taste in his mouth. He knew exactly what this metallic taste was. It was blood and it was plentiful. He looked up and saw the rafters of his condo. He felt a bit better knowing he hadn't been taken to some foreign country, where people could do things to him for days and months without any repercussions.

What didn't make him feel better were the two-inch thick, metal linked chains attached tightly to his wrists. His fingers had turned purple and his hands were numb.

He put some weight on his legs and, staring at his captor, spat more blood on his rug. He felt a loose tooth; he wiggled it with his tongue until it was completely free and then spit it out as well. It clinked across the floor and slid underneath the refrigerator. He looked up and realized his eyes were fuzzy. He tried to blink it away. The focus in his right eye sharpened, but the left became harder and harder to see out of. He realized quickly that it was because it was swelling shut. He looked at the man across from him; he had dark short hair, faint dark stubble, and dark-brown eyes. Nothing about the man or his posture was inviting or calming. He looked at his white dress shirt and dark slacks and laughed. "Who the fuck are you?"

"I know who you are, but you don't know who I am? Seems like one of us is doing something right in our profession."

"You a hitter? You do things for money also?"

Gabriel didn't say anything; he just shook his head no. The man screamed, "You are seriously trying to tell me you aren't doing this for money? You're a lying piece of shit, do you know that?"

Gabriel turned around, keeping a safe distance between himself and the man. He stared at the man and punched him with everything that he had. He hadn't held anything back, and the bones crunched beneath his fist. The man's head snapped backwards. His mouth was open as he screamed in pain; he hadn't hurt like that in years. The blood that poured from his nose gushed into his open mouth, once again becoming the dominant taste. He spat it out and hung his head, squinting as he tried to stop the tears.

Gabriel spoke. "No… I am not here on a paid status. I'm here working pro bono. There will be no payment for this… no seven figures added to my offshore bank account. I came here because I missed the original call, and unfortunately, you were the one that took the job. I got back too late and looked up the hit; it was a woman, plus two. The 'plus two' were both children."

Harry laughed. "Are you trying to tell me that you really think you're above all of this? You follow rules and a code and you won't—"

Gabriel swung the giant phone book in an arc over his head and slammed it full force into the man's gut. The wind left his lungs in a way he'd never felt before. Harry was debating on which was more painful: the broken nose, the fractured jaw, or the pain in his gut.

Gabriel said, "I'm not pure of sin. I'm not perfect. But I don't kill families. I don't kill kids. I don't *ever* kill kids. If you followed that practice, maybe you'd still be able to take that job in Vermont next month."

"Wait! How the hell do you know about Vermont? Where did you find out about that?"

"You're hanging here by chains in your own apartment and your life is in my hands. Yet, you still think you should be underestimating me. You still think, somehow, you are the smarter of the two of us?"

"Well, if you don't want anything from me, then why the hell am I still alive? Why are you toying with me? Why are you torturing me?"

"Oh, I haven't started to torture you yet. I haven't begun to do anything yet. I need something from you. I need you to clarify something for me."

"You're going to get the information from me and kill me. I know it; that's what we do… that's who you are."

Gabriel walked a slow circle around him, evaluating him from behind. He pulled a large sack from his pocket and shook it out. Harry heard the sound, knowing instantly that it was plastic and began screaming and buckling. "What the hell are you doing back there? What are you doing? Tell me now! If you're going to kill me, at least tell me! Don't be a coward—tell me what you are doing! Do you hear me, god damn it? Speak, will you?"

Gabriel walked back around to the front staring at the man, seeing the fear in his eyes. "You are going to tell me who hired you, who you killed."

Harry smiled. "So, you aren't going to kill me? You are going to let me live?"

Gabriel shrugged. "I don't have time for this. Over time, I can get the information that I need. It's going to take me a little longer, but I was trying to speed the process along. I have some work that I need to do and this is just a waste of time."

"Let me live. I'll tell you everything; I swear. I swear on my mother's grave!"

Gabriel pulled a bar stool over and sat in front of him, staring him down. "Harry, I know everything about you. I've done my homework; first off, your mother isn't dead, your father is… but he was a drunk and a man who was not the envy of anyone. You choose to lie to me; you must have a serious death wish. Of course, there is the chance that you are just plain stupid."

Harry shook his head no. "I was going to be done. I was going to get out. After what I made from him, it was all I needed to reside on easy street for the rest of my life. It was that asshole who owns the software company. His guard hired me, but the guy's name was Steven… Steven Riddick. It was his idea. They contracted me to do it; they hired me."

Gabriel looked around. "So, you wanted the big payout, and you were going to get out of the business after this?"

"Yeah man, I was done. I wasn't going to do it anymore. I swear; I do, man. I'm fucking done. Just let me go, and you'll never see or hear from me. You won't have to look over your shoulder. I won't mess with you. I just had that one job in Vermont already scheduled."

Gabriel stared deep into the man's eyes as he slid the

plastic bag over his head. Before he tightened it, Harry screamed, "I told you what you wanted, you lying bastard! You have to let me live! You have to, god damn it!"

Gabriel gripped the man by the hair. "You took the innocent and you have sins to pay for. You can live. By all means, *do*. Remember, I'm not the one killing you; the bag is."

Gabriel put a zip tie around the bag, making it as tight as he could. The man's eyes bugged out of his head. Harry tried to buckle and shake, but there was nothing he could do. He knew he was in a losing position. Gabriel sat back down, staring at the man. He knew he did not need to worry about looking over his shoulder because he never had anyone left to worry about coming after him for revenge. The bag filled with steam and hot air. He watched until the man took his last breath, as his dying moments finally came and went. He knew he had a trip to make to visit Riddick and a bodyguard.

Chapter 5
Unwanted Offers

Langley, Virginia

Frank Fox sat at the table, reading for twenty minutes, never looking up once. He shook his head slowly in astonishment. When he finished, he tossed the folder down and let out a long breath; he felt like he had just gone through hell and back. He stood up with the conviction of a man who had accomplished the impossible. He gripped his short blonde hair. "Jesus, Tony. Where the fuck have you been hiding this guy? Is his name really Gabriel, for god sakes, or was that some kind of sick joke on your part?"

Tony sat back in his seat, shaking his head. "He actually picked that, and, really, it's sadly quite accurate, Frank. If God was going to pick someone to kill on his behalf, there's a good chance Gabriel would be at the top of his list."

Tony rubbed at his tired, hazel eyes. He cursed, stretching his back, jealous of the man twenty-plus years younger than himself. He longed for the days when he had the ability and agility to jump out of a chair like Frank did. He had plenty of missions in his bones that had taken a toll on his body. There wasn't a day that passed that he wasn't reminded of the physical missions he'd been assigned to. The things that he had done for his country felt like a valid trade.

"So, what we have is a master assassin, fucking great. That's what we need isn't it, Tony?" Frank pointed at the folder that detailed all of Gabriel's missions and hits in it. "That guy is a couple of years older than me. What the fuck is he doing retired? I mean, the last time I checked there wasn't a pension plan worth a shit, right? Unless the spooks get a better plan than we do... is that the case?"

"It wasn't really something he talked about; he called me and told me he was out. There wasn't a real long discussion about it. He was pretty pissed about it at the time, to tell you the truth."

"You know what we spend to train these spooks, right?"

"It would make a taxpayer sick, but he was adamant that he was out. You don't appreciate what this guy is like when he is passionate about something. There is no right and wrong. It's just what Gabriel thinks and what he does about it."

"Well, expand, Tony."

"His last job, as you read there, which was successful was in South America. We had a ride ready to go for him." Frank went back to the folder and opened it, reviewing the list and nodded. "Looks like he took out a *Juan Valdez*, who gave the Mexican drug cartel a run for their money in the cocaine trade. He was sending FBI agents back in body bags that were trying to..."

Tony cut him off, not about to listen to someone else give him a recap of what he himself had written. "I've heard the report, Frank. I don't need a recap on it. Christ, I wrote the thing."

"I know, but Jesus, did he really take a shot from a mile away?"

"He didn't, or probably more accurately, *still* doesn't understand the word 'can't', Frank. He knew we lost the ride for him but took the shot, anyway. He still took the shot, signing his own death warrant. He broke into the compound where he slit the leader open and got the asset out."

"So, he knew he was going to be gone. What did he tell you?"

Tony rolled the cigarette between his lips. "He told me that he quit and that if anyone tried to bring him in for a debriefing, he would slit their throat. He said nothing about not making it back, only that if we couldn't keep a ride for him and the man, he was out. He never called in again after that."

Frank slid the phone across the table. "You were his handler. You call him. You know how to get inside his head. Make it happen, Tony—that's an order."

"No. That's a death wish. He was dark before we ever trained him. He came to us full of contempt and ready to kill."

Tony pulled out one additional file and slid it across the table; the one that he hadn't yet read. Tony smiled now, giving Frank the creeps for the first time and putting a damper on his cocky attitude. "Here's his training file."

Chapter 6
Training Day

August 7, 2013

The instructors stood in line as the bus pulled through the final turn, where it would come to a rest on the gravel road at the rear of the farm. The instructors' knowing eyes were hidden by large aviation sunglasses. Each of the men was dressed identically in black military fatigues. Today was Christmas for them as their new batch of recruits was coming and would be there in mere minutes. Then the fun would begin.

The instructors couldn't help but anticipate the things that they would put the men and women through over the coming months. Every one of them would be put under a microscope to make sure that they had what it took to survive in the field. The instructors would never send a man out that wasn't fully prepared to handle all of the situations that could come up. They had to break all of the recruits of the mindset that they were going to be the next James Bond.

The unmarked bus stopped five feet in front of them. The driver released the built-up air brake supply from the suspension and lowered the giant metal transport vehicle. When the bus settled, the doors opened. For the recruits, the doors might as well have been a portal to another dimension. A place and time that would have rules and lessons and training that they never thought possible but would one day depend on to save their lives.

All of the recruits had been selected straight from their second year of college. Two instructors watched them file out, all announcing exactly what school they had been plucked from by the school shirts that they wore. They all had the same slim, athletic build, but with a variety of different skin tones. Instructor Wesenberg leaned over and whispered to Pietras. "I wonder what group of dumbshits they brought us this time."

Pietras fought back a laugh; smiling wasn't something the recruits needed to see. "Seems like they are shipping their balls to them later, by the looks of the men. Christ, I remember when I came through; we were already hard by the time we got off the bus. We also weren't getting all the special treatment these pissants do."

The group lined up next to the bus, looking more than a little confused at the scene before them. Whispers from the recruits ranged from *"Oh shit"* to *"What did I sign up for?"* to *"What do you think they expect us to do here? This is day one? You have got to be fucking kidding me."*

Chief Instructor Clary smiled. "Welcome to the farm, ladies and gentlemen. My name is Instructor Clary. You may, and will, call me Instructor Clary. If you call me anything else, I—or one of my men—will beat you to a pulp. Now put your bags down and step this way, please, and follow me."

The group followed their new instructor warily, unsure what the plan was. In front of the new students were ten men with black cloth bags over their heads. Their hands had been handcuffed behind their backs and they were on their knees in front of what appeared to be shallow dug graves.

Instructor Clary pulled the top off a plastic shipping

crate stamped *CIA* in white bold letters. A row of gleaming black pistols were inside of it. There was one gun for each of the future spooks.

A good-looking man with blonde hair was the first to raise his hand. There was always a first, and the instructors all loved betting to see who the first unfortunate soul would be to do so. The instructors ignored his raised hand. Instructor Wesenberg walked behind the row of new cadets, stopping behind the blonde man. He leaned in, whispering just barely at a point of being audible. "Put your fucking hand down before I snap it off and shove it up your ass."

The nervous young man slowly lowered it, not looking behind him to see whh of the instructors had just threatened him. It took less than ten minutes of being off the bus for the young man to yearn for being back in his seat at his university. "Sorry, sir, I—"

Wesenberg didn't allow him to finish. He walked in front of the man, cutting through him and the man next to him, and elbowed the young man hard in the ribs, knocking the air out of his lungs. He dropped quickly to a knee, sucking in a deep breath. Instructor Pietras walked up, dropped down inches from his face, and screamed, "Well, if you are already on your knees you might as well drop all the way down and give me fifty of them now!"

The young man, who was out of his element and confused, spoke before thinking. "Fifty what, sir?"

"Pushups… Jesus H Christ! What kind of morons are they sending us? Are we that bad off that the CIA, of all places, can't get recruits who are capable of intelligent thoughts?"

Wesenberg, who wasn't about to let Pietras have all the fun, dropped down by the blonde man's face, screaming as well, "Is there a reason you haven't done a god damn push up yet, son? Do you think that you are special? I will bounce your ass out of this class so god damn fast, it will make your fucking head spin!"

Pietras pushed back up, grabbing the man's belt, and with one very muscular arm, assisted the man with his first five. Meanwhile, Wesenberg screamed in the recruit's face, helping him count them off.

"Dumbass." A whisper of a voice came from a young man whose large chest, arms, and legs screamed that he'd been a high school football player. His words granted him the full and undivided attention of Clary, who made a beeline straight for him, bumping a chest twice the size of the kid, making him stumble backwards. The kid took a few steps back and popped back to attention after catching his balance. The rest of the recruits, who'd relaxed a bit in their wait for something to happen, immediately followed suit, getting into a tight respectable resting stance as well.

Clary ripped his sunglasses off and threw them angrily across the distance, smashing the lenses against the side of a nearby shed. He stepped in to the jock's face. Spittle flew from his mouth, as he couldn't get the words out as quickly as he wanted them. He gripped him by his shirt collar, lifting him an inch off the ground. "Who the fuck are you to speak? I know god damn well you aren't Edison or Einstein. Pietras, did we have any on this class list that are fucking geniuses?"

Pietras walked to a clipboard and replied, "Just one, sir, but it sure as hell isn't this pencil dick."

The class looked down the line at each other, obviously knowing that they themselves were not the genius in the group. Clary let go of the boy's shirt and threw him to the ground. "Give me seventy-five and hurry up. I still have work to do today and you guys are just wasting my damn time."

The class watched as the two men did pushups as if their lives depended on it. They rose to their feet with their arms feeling like Jell-O and fought to catch a breath. Clary pointed to the hard-shell case. "Everyone grab a pistol and keep all barrels pointed to the ground. Do not... I repeat *do not* put your finger on the trigger." The group walked in formation to the case of pistols, each of them hesitantly picking one.

"Line up in front of one of these pieces of shit." Clary walked behind each of the bagged men smacking them hard on the back of the head. "Each one of these degenerate bastards was found and convicted of one or more acts of terrorism against The United States."

Pietras held up his pistol. It was identical to those the recruits were holding. He pointed to the side of the gun at the safety switch. "Now I am sure none of you know shit about guns, so this little black thing is called a safety switch. If you flick it down it will make the gun not safe. So, don't point at your face or the face of the recruit next to you. The gun will be safe to point at a terrorist though."

Clary stared at the group, but none dared to ask a question after seeing what happened to those who spoke out of turn. "These men deserve to die. This will be your first test. This test is strictly a pass or fail."

While nine of the recruits were busy thinking and trying to determine who would be the first to disobey and thus fail the test, one man stepped forward out of line. He was slim with a ropey, muscular build and cropped dark-brown hair. He walked towards the bagged men. He had his newly acquired gun pointed down, as instructed, and his finger off of the trigger. The instructors were watching him from the corner of their eyes.

The young man stared at them and when the instructors looked away, a succession of four shots went off and four men fell into their shallow graves, one after another. The young man walked to the middle of the remaining six and emptied his magazine until it fired empty. The smoke from his barrel disappeared into the cool morning fog.

The instructors sprinted, leaving the group unattended. All their young faces were frozen with more questions and emotions than a person could handle. Clary ran to the young man, gripped his arm, and reached for the pistol, yanking it away. Pietras and Wesenberg jumped into the first and second of the ten graves and ripped the masks off the men. Clary put the pistol into the rear of his waistband and jumped into the third hole.

The young man leaned over, staring at the three men working quickly to pull the hoods off, and exposing the thin military-grade helmets that each man was wearing. The other two instructors did the same, working frantically. Clary yelled, "Chuck, Chuck!"

He slapped the man across the face, and he did it hard. The man's eyes opened, staring in disbelief at Clary. The man looked around and noticed the grave that he was currently lying flat in. He jumped, forgetting that his hands and feet were tied and started bucking, trying to free himself. Clary held him down, showing him a knife. "Now, Chuck, I'm going to cut you loose. I need you to sit still for me, buddy, or I'm gonna cut your fucking hand off. You think you can do that for me?"

Chuck nodded his head, breathing heavily and looked ready to kill. He had a rage of fire in his eyes and he wanted to take all of it out on some unlucky recipient. Clary cut his hands loose and then cut the restraints from his feet. The man looked up at the kid, then at Clary. "What the fuck happened, Clary? Did that little son of a bitch actually shoot me?"

Clary pulled a radio from his pocket. "Medics, can you come to the new recruits welcoming station on the east side ASAP?"

Less than two minutes later, ten men were resting on the edges of the graves. Each man was staring at the kid in front of them. One of the men finally had to ask, "What's wrong with you, god damn it? You could have killed someone."

The young man had realized exactly what was going on the moment the first mask was pulled, exposing the helmet and the man's white face. "That was my intention, sir. I wouldn't shoot an instructor on purpose."

Clary walked to the table with Pietras, thumbing through the files. He found a file whose picture matched the man standing there, looking cold and unforgiving. He threw the rest back on the table and started reading it. He spoke quietly, "Jacob August. Christ, that doesn't sound as dark as he looks."

Pietras, who was reading over his shoulder, pointed at the file breakdown of the young man. "It looks like we found our genius, Clary. Jesus, look at his psych eval! Fuck! I bet he made the psych department wet when they saw his file."

Clary stared at Pietras. "Is there something else you could be doing besides peering over my fucking shoulder? Take the recruits to the barracks and then see how they like to run. I'm sure that there is at least one quitter here today. After they find out how little they like to run, go ahead and see how little they like calisthenics, also."

Pietras turned on a heel, realizing he was being dismissed. "Yes sir, I'll get them stowed away and start the assessment immediately. There's going to be a lot of puking today, I hope. God, I love my job!"

Clary ignored him, still reading Jacob's profile. His test numbers were off the chart. At twenty years old, he had enough credits to graduate with a double bachelor's degree. In addition to numerous psychology classes he had taken, he was fluent in Arabic and Persian. He looked down to his next of kin and saw there was an uncle who lived in Iowa that was the closest thing to a relative. He read his psychological profile, which stated he knew right from wrong. He had no remorse, though, and his views on right versus wrong were extremely black and white.

Clary set the folder down, pulling a pack of cigarettes from his pocket. He sat there for a minute thinking that if they could teach this kid, he could be one of the best potential field operatives they've had in years—if not ever. He tapped on the smoke, thinking and realizing that if they didn't take care of this young man and rejected him, he could be the scariest damn thing on the planet to have to worry about.

Wesenberg walked over after the ambulances and medics closed their doors, taking the ten men with them. He rubbed his hands through his hair, thanking God he wasn't one of the ones standing there when those shots were fired. Wesenberg cleared his throat and Clary signaled him to come with his index and middle finger. He said, "They're going to be all right. Rogers might have a slight concussion, but, all in all, we'll come out okay on this."

Clary shook two more smokes from his pack, looking up at Wesenberg and then back at the file; he looked up again, shaking his head. He handed Wesenberg one of the two cigarettes and then lit the second with the one he was still trying to finish. He dropped that one in the grave, putting it out with his shined black boot.   "You know, in fifteen years no recruit has ever done that. This is all about breaking them down and resetting their psyche to handle killing people. Recruits don't come in with the mindset that it's okay to kill. We have to explain it, break them down, and put them back together."

Wesenberg lit his smoke and shook out the match. "He shot ten, not one. He took it upon himself to try to kill every single one of them. He's going to be one scary son of a bitch when we're done with him."

"He is going to be an assassin, if I've ever seen one. Screw wet work; he's a natural-born killer. The type that pulls the trigger and just keeps on going without needing the mandatory cool off period. He'll just line them up and keep on knocking them down."

*****

Pietras pushed the group until he thought they were going to break. He had been a track star many moons ago and could still kick the shit out of anyone in a race. He had not yet raced up against Jacob August, though. Jacob and Pietras kept a pace that blew the rest out of the pack. The difference was when Pietras looked like he was about to have organ failure, Jacob was still pumping hard and breathing easy. Jacob looked over, seeing the defeat on his soon-to-be mentor's face and realized that he was going to be put on a serious shit list.

When they finished the run, Pietras bent over, heaving hard. Only Jacob was able to see this, as the others were still a few miles back. Pietras walked over to him, grabbed him by the wrist, and yanked him down to the ground. "You… you tell anyone… anyone, anything about this, I swear to God… you won't ever have to worry about seeing your last day here. I'll bounce your ass from this class!"

Jacob pushed up and knelt in front of him. He said, "Sir, you can kick me out, but you would be ruining the only thing that I got going. You don't understand where I came from or why I'm here. But if I were you, sir, I don't think I would want to be the sole person responsible for putting an end to my only way to get back at those I hate most in life. They took everything from me. If you do take that from me, you will be the next person in my sights."

Pietras looked up, finally catching his breath. "You're a cocky little fuck, aren't you? You realize what threatening an instructor can do to your career? You know I just need to make one phone call, right? I tell instructor Clary and—"

Jacob cut him off, getting as close as he dared to his new teacher's face. "You and I aren't getting off on the right foot here, Instructor Pietras. I am younger; I'm a track star from my college. That probably isn't something you know about me. Something else about me is that I'm here to learn. I'm here to learn to kill and that's it. I will kill without remorse, and if you can teach me those things, I'll do whatever you want. But if you're going to be too bent up over the next few months about the fact that someone twenty years younger than you can outrun you… well then, for your sake, I think maybe you should try and stay the fuck out of my way, sir."

Pietras smiled, hearing the rest of the group coming up

the beaten path in the forest. "You just keep your mouth shut, if you know what's good for you."

The other nine cadets reached them, coming to a stop. They were walking slowly at first until they stood hunched over, their stomachs resting on their knees. The majority of the young faces blew chunks everywhere. Whatever they had left in their stomachs was now spread everywhere. Pietras got his form back and looked as sharp as he had before they started their run. He took a deep breath, making sure he himself was not going to puke, and yelled, "What? Did that make you maggots tired? Christ, I thought we had some Marines in this group. Aren't you supposed to be tough sons of bitches? Everyone drop and do pushups. When I get back, we're going to spend some time on the mat and see if any of you actually know how to do anything useful besides hold your dick."

One of the men stepped forward, arm raised. "How many pushups did you want us to do, sir?"

Pietras walked away without answering. Before he went inside the cabin he yelled, "I don't remember giving you a number, dumbshit! It means you do pushups until I come back. We're going to make sure we have nothing but the fittest operatives standing in front of us. Now drop and push until I come back. If anyone has any questions about it, then maybe you should wait until someone comes back that gives a flying fuck!"

*****

Jacob dropped down and began doing his endless count of pushups. One of the men in the group grunted out a question to him as they began their second test. "What the hell, are you some sort of track star? Christ, you guys were so far ahead of us and you don't even look like you broke a sweat."

Jacob ignored him and just kept doing as he had been directed. He wasn't positive but was pretty sure that if there was going to be mat hand-to-hand instruction, Pietras was going to be requesting a few minutes of his time. The man next to him was not very patient waiting for the answers and asked a little louder. "Why the hell are you trying so hard on the first day? You trying to make everyone here look bad? You think that you are something special? You think you're better than us?"

Jacob kept pushing, never stopping. He looked over at the man. "Don't worry about me, alright? I'm just keeping to myself; I won't be in anyone's way."

"What makes you think you can stay out of my way?"

Jacob gave him as serious a face as he could. "You don't understand. I'll be so far ahead of anyone else that you won't have to worry about me being in your way."

Pietras came back out, ready to teach the class a few more things about pain. He sat watching for a moment. He could see those that were tired and those that could most likely do pushups until the end of time. He stared at his least favorite, Jacob, and saw the "end of time" look on his face. He had to get past the fact that he didn't like the kid. He knew exactly how good someone like this could be. "Alright ladies, that's enough pushups. Now let's go to the workout facility; we're going to learn so much today."

One of the women raised her hand as they walked. Pietras nodded to her and she said, "Sir, I don't appreciate you calling everyone in the group ladies as if you mean that women are weak."

Pietras nodded as he walked away. "Sorry about that. Maybe you thought you got off the bus in the land of make believe, where your instructors give a fuck, ma'am."

He walked into the barn and opened the doors wide to keep it from getting too hot inside. He flicked a switch and the lights around the raised platform shone down on it. Pietras motioned to the bleachers and the group started to head over to it. He yelled, "Jacob, I think that you're going to be my sparring partner today. Why don't you get up in the ring and see if we can't teach you something that might save your life one day."

Jacob rolled his neck and shoulders, trying to get a little feeling back in his joints after the run and the insane number of pushups. He climbed up the three steps where Pietras was already walking around. He was shaking his arms loose, though they were not burdened with the feeling of a hundred-plus pushups. He said, "You ready to learn something, Jacob? Do you know the first rule to fighting for your life?"

Jacob walked slowly towards him, keeping four feet between them, and walking a slow circle. He held his hands up flat and open. Pietras walked the circle with him holding his weathered, old, and scarred knuckles that were white from being squeezed too hard. Pietras thought again that his years of experience were going to be valuable. He couldn't help himself when it came to underestimating the recruits. The majority of them came in with a high IQ and in decent physical condition, but they also didn't know their fighting skills from their assholes.

The two men circled for a moment. When the rest of the instructors came in, Wesenberg yelled, "You going to teach him something, Pietras? Or you going to check his diaper and see if he shit himself?"

Pietras released the pressure on his knuckles for a second to lift up his middle finger. He put his focus back on Jacob, who didn't respond. "You see, the problem with fighting for your life is you have to want to live *and* not want to live. Does that make sense to you, son? Can you understand what I'm saying here?"

Jacob shrugged. "I might have more problems then. I don't worry about living or dying, as long as I take out those who have made others hurt. Or if I can keep them from hurting others."

"Jesus, you're just a damn boy scout, aren't you? Kind of a dark one, though."

When Jacob shrugged this time, Pietras sent a well-aimed punch straight towards his nose. Jacob saw the instructor's shoulder move before he had a chance to throw it. Jacob stepped to the right and pushed the man's arm into the air with his right hand. With his left hand, Jacob sent two palm strikes. The first went into his ribs and the second into his chest, knocking Pietras back a foot and off balance. As Pietras started to stumble, Jacob spun on his left foot; with his right foot, he sent a reverse sidekick to the man's chest, knocking him off his feet and to the ground. Clary tapped Wesenberg on the shoulder and nodded his head to go up. "We don't let our own get their asses kicked—get up there; we need to teach. Don't hurt him where he is outclassed for too long, but teach him."

Wesenberg smiled quickly, nodded, unbuttoned his black fatigue jacket, and tossed it on the ground. He jumped up on the platform, spacing himself a few feet away. The three men made a perfect triangle. Wesenberg said, "You see, son, it's not always going to be one-on-one, and in cases like that, you need to either learn how to take on two men, or learn how to take a beating. Which one do you want it to be, son?"

Jacob thought of his father, and the lack thereof, in his life and said, "I'd like to be able to take care of two-on-one, sir."

Wesenberg smiled and said, "Well, maybe over time you might have an opportunity to do such a thing."

Jacob kept his hands up without backing up; Wesenberg lunged at him with a front snap kick to the face. Jacob stepped to the side, reached in and underneath Wesenberg's leg. He pushed the older man's foot into the air. He then unleashed a palm strike to the nose, feeling and seeing the blood all at once. Pietras came running, but Jacob was already in motion. He swung in a circle, holding on to the bleeding Wesenberg and not letting go until he was perfectly aimed to fall into Pietras' path. Pietras tried to change his pace, but as he did, he was flying into the air, tripping over

Wesenberg. Jacob caught him in midair, gripping the back of the instructor's fatigues, and rammed his knee into his gut.

Jacob looked at the two men, both writhing in pain and both staring at him confused. Neither of the men were strangers to a beating, but neither of them had ever taken such a brutal one on the first day of training. They were amazed at how quickly it had happened. Clary walked up smiling at Jacob, clapping slowly. He looked down at his two instructors in disgust, leaving no doubt in their minds that there would be one hell of a tongue-lashing later as they sat in the instructors' apartment, nursing their wounds with whiskey. "Instructor Pietras and Wesenberg, I suggest that you sit the rest of this out; I will go about finishing the mat training for the day."

He walked up to Jacob and looked at the rest of the class, feeling bad about what he needed to do. Clary knew he could lose the entire class if they were not shown who was in charge and who was the alpha here. He waited at the edge of the mat for the two instructors to sit on the bleachers with the rest of the class, where they could lick their wounds. Jacob started to walk in slowly, but Clary held up a finger. "Just one more minute. Let's let the instructors get situated so they can get some training as well. Seems to me that they have forgotten some of the many things that they've learned over the years."

Jacob walked to the edge of the mat, making sure he kept plenty of distance between himself and the man that was much shorter than he was, but much stronger. Clary waited patiently until the two had their seats and then turned around cracking his neck and stretching his fingers. He too made fists and came in with a boxer's approach. Jacob kept walking backwards towards the edge. Unlike Pietras, Clary didn't underestimate the young man. He kept his chin down and walked at an angle, knowing that the smaller he kept himself, the harder it was to hit him. Jacob waited for him and when he threw the first punch, he slid to the side bringing a leg up for the man's head. Clary backtracked a step, gripping

Jacob's thigh, lifting him up off the ground, and slamming him with every bit of force that he had down on the mat.

Jacob tried to roll, but Clary kept him in place with an iron grip around his shoulder. He dealt two mind-numbing punches to Jacob that left him dazed and dizzy. For the briefest moment, Clary looked up to see if he had the class' respect back and in that millisecond, a knife-hand strike to his throat took away his ability to breathe. Clary gripped his throat as a natural reaction and when he did, Jacob used every bit of muscle in his leg to flip the man off of him, over his head, sending him into the air, and landing on his back. The hit further took air out of him and Clary rolled to his side, seeing nothing but red. He climbed back on the mat. Jacob pushed back up to his feet, staggering backwards and shaking off what was left of his dizziness.

Clary made a conscious decision that he wouldn't take his eyes off of the young man again. If he was around, his eyes would be on him. Jacob approached this time, and when he did, Clary left him standing patiently, not sure what to expect from the surprising young man. Jacob lifted a foot, as if to kick low; as he extended his foot, Clary was ready for it. Jacob then surprised him by jumping off his standing foot, spinning in the air, and connecting it to the side of his instructor's head. Clary tried to back up and give himself a moment, but Jacob was on him, delivering massive knockout punches; one, two, three punches from the young man. Clary could see the lights starting to go dark, but before they did, he ran up, taking more punches and bear hugged Jacob, squeezing him tighter than he had known was possible.

Clary ran a few steps back with him, making sure he was perfectly in place to finish the kid. He whispered, "You got heart kid. You are going to be fucking great one day."

He brought his head back and then snapped it forward into Jacob's, leaving him dazed as blood poured from a new cut across his forehead. He released the young man and sent a palm strike of his own into Jacob's chest. Jacob stumbled backwards and was gone; to prove his point to the student and the rest of the class watching, he sent one size-twelve boot into the young man's groin and then a knee into his face, flattening the less-experienced Jacob out. Jacob watched blurrily as the instructor stood over him while the lights from the barn swayed back and forth. The room spun until he finally blacked out. Pietras and Wesenberg looked at each other, only mildly amused, knowing that if he had taken out Clary, there would be nothing left to try to teach the students. They would think one of their own already knew more than the instructors.

Clary wiped at blood on his own face and pointed to the student sprawled on the ground. "This is a great lesson to be had. You must keep their hands off you. I don't care how many of them there are; you make sure you do. Once they get a hand on you, your balance is thrown, your distance of keeping yourself safe is off, and there is little, if anything, that you can do to get away. When multiple assailants are attacking you, you need to be confident in your abilities, but when outmatched, you also need to know when to run. Sometimes running can keep you from looking at things from the flat of your back. Going forward, take in as much as you can learn. We don't learn on the job here. We don't try and hope you learn from your mistakes. Once you leave here, you die. You don't learn to live another day. You will be, in most cases, on your own and if you fuck up, you die. If this sounds harsh, I'm doing my job. There is nothing we can do for you once you leave here; there is no further advice that we can give you and nothing that we can do to save you. If they don't kill you, then one thing you can be very confident of is the horrible ways they'll torture you; they will do it in every way possible until they think they have every bit of knowledge extracted from you that they can get." Clary stared at the young faces with a smile and said, "Everyone still thinking that leaving college at twenty-one was a good idea? If you aren't nervous now, you're stupid. If you are, then you just might stand a chance."

He looked at his two instructors sitting on the bleachers like the rest and yelled, "Is there a reason they are still sitting on bleachers? They look like they are just dying to take a run around the lake!" Pietras got up and glanced at Jacob lying on the mat, "You think he's up for a run, sir?"

"No, I think he's had enough for a bit. I think that he earned a break teaching his instructors a valuable lesson on underestimating a recruit on day one. It was surely a mistake that will never happen again."

Both men nodded, stretching their backs out and Pietras bellowed, "Get the fuck up and get out that door before I kick the shit out of every last one of you! Move! Move! Move! Do it now!"

The class exploded out the door. They took their time running this time, none of them quite sure if they would be running their last run of the day. Pietras ran in front again, showing the recruits what an old man was capable of. He said a little prayer that Jacob was out for this run and that he wouldn't be someone that he needed to try and best. Wesenberg took the behind position in the run, screaming at the top of his lungs every time someone thought they could for one minute slow down.

Clary walked over rolling, his shoulders, feeling the match between himself and the much younger man. "You doing all right, August? Do you need to go to the medic or do you think some bunk time would be enough?"

Jacob pushed himself to sit up, shaking his head. He could feel the warm blood dripping down his face and disappearing into his black shirt. A drop of it hit his eye, making it sting. He pulled his shirt up to wipe at his forehead. "You always this hard on new recruits?"

Clary smiled and walked up, holding a hand out to pull Jacob up. "To tell you the truth, yes, yes I am. I don't usually bring it quite so hard on the first day, but no one has ever gotten one over on Pietras and Wesenberg before. Usually they'll send someone to the infirmary with a broken rib or nose depending on how they feel about the recruit. Good chance that was exactly what they were attempting with you. It kind of looks like you went and fucked up their plans, didn't you?"

"So, that's how you teach recruits? You beat the shit out of them until they are brought into submission?"

"You hunt, August?"

"That isn't what I asked. I said..."

"I don't give a flying fuck what you asked. I asked *do you hunt*?"

Jacob shook his head slowly. Clary said, "Well, I've been bird hunting since I was able to walk a hill. Now, if you take out a dog and you don't teach it respect, you lose its respect for its entire life. Now do you think you can effectively teach something that doesn't have the utmost respect for you, or at the very least, the fear in what they can and will do for you?"

Jacob opened his mouth, but it was just what Clary was waiting for. "I know that we might not have your respect. You came out of the night and no one knows anything about you, other than you are here to learn some seriously scary shit. Now the rest of the class is still watching everything with puppy dog eyes and needed to be gripped by the neck and choked out for a minute. They needed to know who was in charge and that they need to respect those that were leading. I think that happened, while it might be shitty for you, there was no other way. Now get your ass to the bunks and catch some shuteye. If you decide that you need some medical attention, I highly suggest that you go and do it."

Jacob stared the man in the face. "If I stay here, you'll be able to teach me? You'll be able to make sure I have the skill set that I need to survive and to take out those that don't deserve to live?"

Clary nodded his head. "If you'll listen and learn, we can make you the scariest son of a bitch that the enemy has ever seen."

Jacob nodded, turned around slowly, and headed to the bunks where he could relax and heal and come back stronger and more prepared. He had every intention of being more ready than anyone that they've ever had in their class before.

Chapter 7
Another Day

October 1, 2024

Gabriel sat at a traffic light looking around, checking his rear view, and realized he was being more cautious than need be—if there was such a thing. He had a job to do today: a high-profile gig that would set him up for the rest of the year, even if he were to spend money at a rate that would make a banker cringe. He drove down a desolate street in a part of town that didn't have much going for it except bank-owned bankruptcy properties and his own small, abandoned warehouse. Back when he had a handler, he had purchased this piece of property for himself under the name of a shell corporation.

Gabriel hit the remote for his garage door and waited as it slid up. He pulled in, parked quickly, and went to the doorway, where he hit the close button and punched in a security code. He glanced at the squares of C4 fastened to the sides of the walls. The light went green and he turned around, walking backwards as he watched the red lights everywhere turn green again. He thought of the people coming in that didn't belong here, and that the flashing red lights would be the absolute last thing they ever would see.

Gabriel got back in the truck and put it in line with his other cars that he kept there. He had a collection of rusty, old work trucks, beater cars, an ambulance, and some vans that had a collection of interchangeable signs he could put on them. He walked to the side of a green van and attached a magnetic sign, which read *Lambert Elevator Repair and Sons, Since 1908*. He turned the engine over to make sure it was still running topnotch and then turned it off again. His life depended on its reliability. He walked up to the changing room where he kept changes of clothes, depending on the job.

Gabriel turned on the lights, and they flickered on their yellowish-green tint, filling the room. He went to the locker labeled *Elevator Repair* and opened the door. Gabriel checked his watch. He still had two hours to spare so he took his time going over his plan. He logged into his computer; there was little time for people to back out, but if he was doing a local job, he always made a habit of checking. His fastidiousness cost him nothing and could very well save his life one day.

The laptop, which was as secure as any computer could be, fired up and came to life. Gabriel waited patiently for the password code box to display itself. When it presented the space to type in the words, he typed in his sister's first name, her middle initial, and the date of her and his parents' funeral. He knew that he would never ever forget something as dear to him as that day. He tapped in the keys carefully and punched the enter key.

He sat back while it loaded, bringing up the yellow biohazard symbol. It cast a yellow glow across his crisp, white shirt and turned his face an unhealthy-looking shade of lime. He brought up the website that managed the transactions and jobs. He went to the day's date and typed in more commands. He verified on the page that there were no cancellations; there was only a short two-word message typed in green, saying *good luck*. He shut it down and put it back in his briefcase.

Gabriel thought over everything; he was ready and didn't have any reservations to worry about. His research on the mark was solid, and there could be no better intel because he had done it himself, as he always did. He thought about the drive ahead of him; he was going to have to drive slow or risk getting there much too early. He refused to stay in the silent warehouse for a long period of time, though. If he did, the quiet would win and eventually he would begin to think. He would think until the demons and ghosts made their way into his head. He knew that getting them back out again was not a task to be done lightly.

He stood from the bench, unbuttoning his white dress shirt one button at a time. He laid the clothes neatly in a burn bin next to the lockers and then carried it over to a ventilation shaft. He doused it with a generous amount of gasoline, not wanting to leave anything behind. He was unworried about the SUV because he'd wiped it out clean before coming to the warehouse, as he did every time he had a job near home. The truck would be traced back to no one. The VIN on it was lost long ago in the motor vehicle registration. He knew that he was being overly cautious, that the chances of someone coming in and diffusing all of the bombs before they went off would be near impossible. If they were able to keep this from happening, that meant there were many people there. The only way they would be able to accomplish such a feat would be to move with military precision and speed. He knew that there was an even smaller chance that they would be able to find the ones that weren't out in the open. This number, of course, outnumbered the ones that were visible.

He pulled out a pack of matches and set the clothes ablaze, letting them burn as he watched the flames dance into the shaft until there was nothing but a smoldering pile of ashes. Gabriel pulled a pair of dirty blue overalls out of the classic tan lockers. The overalls smelled like he'd done the job every day for twenty years and that he'd worn this same pair, unwashed, the entire time while chain smoking. He brushed some of the overalls' grease on his face and forehead and messed up his hair a little before putting on a cap that covered up his short-cropped hair.

He opened a trunk and looked at a small personal

armory. This was what kept him alive in times of danger. He pulled out a harness and slid it on, tightening its leather straps over his shirt. He put silenced pistols into the leather holsters, clicking them tight. He hid knives everywhere that he was able to; people who underestimated the weapons usually ended up dead. He attached magazines across his body and on the harness as well. He prayed that there would be no reason to try and use this many, knowing that if he did, something would have gone horribly wrong.

Gabriel went to the van, taking a quick walk to check that everything looked in place and then double-checked the sign. He slid his elevator repair toolbox into the vehicle and got behind the wheel. Gabriel headed across town, taking his time and making sure to obey the traffic laws. He thought of the insane price he had placed on the kill and realized they truly wanted this man dead if they were this serious about paying his fees. He typically wasn't about to do anything so radical when it came to a fee, but the day after he had begun his client's contract he saw that the man had been taken in by the FBI.

He had sent the client his price already, but sent a new figure when he had realized the probability that he was going to have to do something with a federal building. He didn't like changing a contract once a price had been negotiated. He, however, was not stupid to what would happen to himself if he was caught while trying to do the job. Assassins were not the most popular people in the world. He knew from experience what they would do to a hitter if he were caught. He'd found it a little strange that when he had told the client that he was going to have to raise the price they accepted immediately. Gabriel actually contemplated that maybe he should have asked for more. It seemed the second he sent the request to up the price and ask if they wanted to continue with the job, the client had already been typing the word "yes" in response.

Gabriel checked his GPS and saw he was only two

blocks away when he stopped on a side street. He did a final check in the mirror, looking at the ensemble and trying out a thick Russian accent for good measure. When he quit staring at himself in the mirror, he looked out the van's cracked front window. He craned his neck at the hotel, which was tall enough that it looked like it could disappear into the blue sky.

He usually wouldn't put himself in these types of situations, but he was aware that was what gave him the ability to charge such insane prices. Anyone can kill for a living, but the difference between a guy that makes five grand for killing a cheating husband and a guy that can take a half-mile shot between two buildings, comes down to one thing: skills. Gabriel had them and he was marketing them brilliantly. He knew how this would go down. He would sneak into the hotel and make his hit on a federally protected witness.

Gabriel knew when he read the fact sheet about the man that there was one sure thing—that was going to be the end of him. Gabriel knew just looking at pictures of the man on the internet that he was a long-time smoker and he would be in need of one eventually; without a doubt, the itch for nicotine would get under the man's skin. So, Gabriel watched the building long enough to discover the time and the spot they took those that couldn't keep the habit at bay. It worked out perfectly with the hotel because it was going to be when it was at its quietest. The previous day's guests would be gone by now and the new ones would not yet be ready to check in, leaving the floors filled with people. They would not care why a repairman was there or what he was doing.

Gabriel put the van back in drive, closing the distance and took it around to the back where the workers and vendors parked. He knew that a member of the staff would have a heart attack if he tried to go through the front door of the building.

He checked his watch out of habit, knowing that he wasn't running late, but he didn't have time to waste. He left the van running, got out, slid the large door open, and grabbed the long toolbox that held the "masterpiece to his Picasso". He peered around the lot, pretending to be fumbling with items in his van. He knew his outs if he wasn't able to take the van with him and hated the idea of leaving on foot. Having a federal building across the street just means it would be like flies on shit in a matter of moments; that made being up so many flights an unappealing thing.

He grabbed the heavy toolbox and walked up to the two rear doors and punched the buzzer. He painted an expression over his face that said he couldn't give two shits if he did this job or not since there would be a long list of them yet to follow. A young man, probably no more than twenty-one, opened the door holding a clipboard filled with the day's expected appointments. It was not going to have Gabriel's repair on it. He stared at Gabriel, trying to remember the practiced line that he was in charge of saying. By the look on the young man's face, Gabriel thought there was a good chance he was not operating at a full mental capacity right now. The young man finally stammered, "What are you here to fix today?"

Gabriel tapped on his chest with one finger, putting on the thick accent. "Elevator."

"Do you have an appointment?"

Gabriel rolled his eyes and shrugged. He laid on the accent pretty thick and said, "Look, my English is no great. My boss said to come to the Taylor Hotel. This is Taylor Hotel, yes?"

The kid nodded. "Yes, you have the right hotel."

"My boss say 'stop, fix real quick… in and out, then you go home'. I cannot go home until you let me in so I can fix what needs fixed."

The kid looked up and down the list. "I don't see you anywhere on this, like at all."

Gabriel shrugged, really laying down how little he cared. "When did you print list?"

The kid looked at it and said out loud without meaning to, "Oh hell. Well, this damn thing was printed at six in the fucking morning. How the hell do they expect us to keep track of you guys coming and going all damn day if we don't even know that you're coming? I mean, how hard is it to print it more than once, or to update it? They want to keep the place safe, but they don't want to put any effort into it."

Gabriel nodded, acting like he didn't know it was a rhetorical question. "I do not know this answer? Maybe not hard to do? I am not so good with computer. It is why I fix elevator."

The kid nodded slowly and then laughed, realizing that the man didn't know he wasn't supposed to actually answer. Gabriel looked at his watch and then back up, smiling. "Seems like you work for a urod."

The kid snapped his head up. "A what?"

Gabriel held up his hand in apology, waving it up and down. "I slipped, sorry, uh… how do you say… moron…? Yes. You work for a moron… a real, uh, dipping shit."

The kid got a momentary look of anger on his face and then laughed, realizing how exactly right the foreign man was. "Yeah, you know, that is a pretty accurate description."

The kid pushed the door fully open for Gabriel, motioning him in and looking around the parking lot. When Gabriel didn't move, he motioned him through with his hand. "There is a maintenance stairwell you can use. I assume if the elevators are acting up, you don't want to take them, right?"

Gabriel nodded his head. "Well, it wouldn't get fixed anytime soon if I got stuck in the elevator, would it?"

The kid held out a clipboard and a visitor badge. Gabriel set the toolbox down on a table and took the clipboard, scribbling a messy signature on the board that said *John F Kennedy*. He left grease stains on it when handing it back to the man. Later when they tried to look at the clipboard to get prints, they would pull perfect ones that had been bought in the best shop in Tokyo to a man that no one

knew, because he didn't exist. Gabriel confirmed the
direction that the man had pointed in and headed that way
after seeing him nod. He could hear the kid repeating *urod* in
the background and was confident someone was going to be
hearing that from him someday without being privy to the
meaning.

He squeezed past other workers as he made his way to
the back where the kid had pointed. He thought about the
spacious entryways that all hotels had and the lavish rooms
with vaulted ceilings and how it was all elegance and beauty
until you were forced to go to the back of the hotel, where
everything that was in there had a purpose and a duty. He
knew that if it didn't belong there, it wouldn't have been put
in place because they needed to be as efficient as possible.

When a few employees tried to speak to Gabriel, he
mumbled sentences in Russian, knowing that there was a slim
chance anyone was going to be replying back to him. He
could tell from their own accents that they probably spoke a
tongue that was not native to this land as well. But from his
time abroad, he knew they were speaking Bosnian. Most
employees didn't try very hard to speak to him because the
only thing that the employees hated worse than the guests that
stayed here were the workers from outside companies that
came into their building and didn't know their language.

Gabriel thought about the steps and realized that
sometimes the elevator gig was not the greatest idea, knowing
that he was going to be climbing up fifteen flights of stairs,
which wasn't something that excited him. He took the steps
two at a time, his long legs making short work of them. He
knew that he could run the damn things with the heavy
toolbox and still not be out of breath by the time he made it
up the steps. But he also knew that if someone saw a man
over six feet tall, dirty and greasy, and running with a toolbox
and an elevator repair sign on his back, it might make guests
and employees more than just a little nervous. He did enjoy
jobs where people would ask him if he thought that it was

safe to ride it up and down. He would smile and say, "Well, yes, you can, but I think you'll live longer if you take the stairs or take elevator on other side of building."

Gabriel enjoyed using that line the most. The awkward smiles of nervousness that he got back were the best, almost priceless. He made it to the flight that he required to complete his job. He put his ear to the door, listening for a moment, trying to make sure there was no one in the hallway. The more people that he was able to avoid the better. Gabriel opened the door slowly, looking both ways. He knew there would be no intelligent reason why an elevator repairman would be walking up and down the halls of the hotel.

Gabriel made it to the room he wanted to use. He had a total of five that he knew would work if this one ended up being occupied. He kept an eye on the hall, and when he was sure no one was coming, he slid in a key card that had a ribbon coming out of it. This was connected to a smart phone that started a software program and went through millions of algorithms in an extremely short amount of time. The red light on the door stayed red for a moment until it switched to green and the door's lock clicked, allowing Gabriel into the room.

Gabriel quickly put the toolbox down and, from his overall's pocket, pulled a plastic zip tie like officers and DEA agents used to secure people instead of metal handcuffs. He stretched as far as he could, putting it around the door's mechanism that kept it from slamming. He pulled the zip tie shut tight, ensuring no one would be able to open the door unless they removed it with a battering ram or a bomb to completely remove it from its frame.

Gabriel tried the handle to make sure it wasn't able to budge. He nodded, reassured that he would have all the privacy he required until he removed it. Gabriel moved through the suite, making sure there was no cleaning lady bent over a toilet with an iPod, missing all of the excitement and oblivious to the fact that he was there. After clearing the place, he was reassured that no one else was in the room with him and he returned to his toolbox. He opened the rusty lid and pulled out a long shelf of tools to reveal a much deeper, longer space beneath. He looked inside, admiring a rifle broken down into three pieces, as well as a high-powered scope. They were all fit into a perfectly cut, molded foam piece.

Gabriel checked his watch, thinking of the man and knowing that he was going to be needing that smoke in a half hour or less. He removed a suction cup from the toolbox and attached it to the south window in the room. He screwed a metal diamond-edged glasscutter to the center of the suction cup's handle. Gabriel took it around the edge of the glass. The only thing currently able to break his concentration was the sound of glass on glass being cut. He was not a fan of the sound and couldn't think for the life of him who would be. When he made his way all the way around, he was rewarded with not having to hear the noise anymore. He set the glass, still attached to the suction cup, on the bed.

Gabriel pulled the three pieces of the rifle out, connecting the barrel to the upper and lower and connected the stock of the rifle to the receiver. He slid the scope into place and locked it. He then slid the last two things that he needed into place: a bi-pod and a full magazine. He pulled back the charging handle and set it down on the ground. He opened the blinds a little more than a foot, leaving the room almost completely engulfed in black. He used the two books, which were guaranteed to be in the room, on each side to keep the blinds from flapping in the wind from the freshly cut hole. He placed the Bible on one and the phone book on the other. Gabriel walked to the other end of the room and lay down in a practiced shooter's position. He adjusted the rifle until it was a part of him and got into a position that he knew, come hell or high water, he would not move from until he had accomplished his job.

Gabriel adjusted his scope until he could read the

words on the building a half-mile away that read "Dispose of your butts". He checked his watch one last time, knowing he had only minutes before the job would be completed. He sat patiently until his alarm went off; when it did, he pressed it, set it aside, and watched his mark come out onto the stone patio a few minutes later. The man was in a polo shirt that looked like he'd been wearing it for a few days and a pair of jeans. He was handed a cigarette from one of the two guards accompanying him, both dressed in identical black suits. The man lit the much-needed smoke, pulled hard on it, and let out a long, steady stream of smoke.

Gabriel smiled, knowing it would be the last drag he took unless heaven allowed it. He zeroed in, seeing his shot, and sent his bullet the half-mile between the hotel and the federal building down the street. It took the bullet just over a second from the time the report echoed to make its way to where Gabriel had it aimed. The .308 round punched into the man standing on the balcony. Gabriel never lifted his eye from the scope.

He stared at the man, knowing that he didn't miss. But then he didn't ever miss. Gabriel shot true and straight and he never questioned his aim. He expected to paint the wall behind the man red with his own insides. He thought he would see the concrete behind him explode as the bullet tore through the mark. Instead of this happening, he simply stumbled backwards against the wall.

Gabriel smiled, thinking of the price he'd charged, and felt even less bad now about the fact that he'd raised it so high. He was thinking of letting the person know that this had officially become a huge pain in his ass. He blamed the FBI but wasn't sure why. He couldn't blame someone if they knew they had a price on their head and did nothing to at least try and keep the inevitable from happening. The fact that the bullet did not go through the man's body armor did little about the force that it came at him with. It had nowhere to go with the vest in the way, and the power with which it punched him was incredible. It didn't knock the man on his ass, but it was close.

Gabriel thought of the rifle in his hands and wished it were a fifty-caliber rifle instead. If that were the case, the kinetic energy from the gun would have still torn the man in half. Unfortunately, a fifty-caliber rifle would never have fit into the rusty metal toolbox. He knew if he carried anything much bigger than that, he was going to look ridiculous and start to draw attention that he didn't need.

The two FBI agents that were standing on the balcony with him immediately drew their pistols, which at a half of a mile, could have been slingshots for all the good they would have done them. Gabriel looked through the concrete railing that made up the balcony. The man he'd shot lay on the ground and, while not dying, he was most definitely writhing in pain. He had his hands clutched to his chest, holding the spot where the bullet had collided with him. He shifted his focus to the two men dressed in black suits. They were listening and screaming into their wrists. Gabriel focused on the man, and when he tried to sit up, one of the two men jumped on top of him, knocking him back to the ground.

Gabriel got the man's head in his cross hairs, thinking it unfortunate that the agent protecting his assignment wouldn't be returning home. Gabriel did not like to take out those that he wasn't being paid to kill, but if someone was in the way, then it was a risk that person took by taking the job. He squeezed the rifle's trigger, knowing there would already be men in the area looking for the shooter.

He was confident that pulling the trigger a second time was as good as calling them and giving them directions to where he was. The second bullet cut through the air above the unsuspecting onlookers twenty floors below. They were staring around in confusion at the gunfire taking place. The bullet sped with an unforgiving force towards its destination. When the bullet got near the end of its path, it tore through the side of the mark's skull. The unfortunate agent was even worse. He was at such an angle that it went through his jaw and out of the top of his skull. The man's face exploded; his teeth, looking like small white mints glimmering in the midday sun, flew everywhere. His skull was mangled and the two men's blood and brain matter painted the last man standing, leaving a silhouette of blood and gore on the back of the wall.

After the second shot, the remaining protection agent was stunned, staring in shock for a moment as he looked at his assignment and partner sprawled across the ground in a bloody entanglement. He grabbed a pair of binoculars from a case left on the roof and immediately began scanning across the street from behind a pillar that he thought was sufficient cover. Within a moment, he was staring directly at Gabriel's hole in the window. He adjusted the optics until the focus was crystal clear and he was sure about what he was seeing. The agent reached his wrist up to his mouth, and as he was about to speak, the left binocular shattered; the third and final bullet blasted through his eye, into his skull, and this time decimated the brick wall behind him. The man's head snapped backwards and his knees and the rest of his body went limp beneath him.

Gabriel scanned the rest of the buildings top and front, guaranteeing there were no riflescopes being trained on him. He did not check the mark a last time because he knew without question that the man would be attending no courtrooms. The chances of him testifying anytime soon were nonexistent. Gabriel never felt bad for the marks, because it wasn't the way he operated. He knew in this case that if the mark would have just kept his mouth shut the now-deceased William Belyeu could have had a lucrative and long career as a talented CPA for one of the largest independently owned corporations in America.

Gabriel had done his normal investigating, taking a quick look to see who actually hired him. Gabriel was told that his website that had jobs listed was impenetrable, but that was only true for the average computer user. In Gabriel's line of work, the intel was almost as important as the hit itself. He found that the man who had hired out the job was Ted Nulty, one of the most powerful men in America. He owned the company and was its president. There was no board; he did not want or need help running his own company. Nulty was in his seventies and still going strong. He had been avoiding the FBI for years, as no one on the inside was stupid enough to give up federal incriminating evidence on him and his company.

From what his reports said about the man, Ted Nulty was a ruthless man who took nothing for granted. He had grown up with nothing, making his fortune the old-fashioned way. When he had heard about a CPA that was about to turn evidence on him, Gabriel figured that was when he put out a hit on Mr. William Belyeu. Gabriel knew that Ted hadn't worked seventy hours a week for decades just to lose his empire and have nothing to pass on to his family when he was gone.

Worried what might happen to him if his recorded deposition was on file, William remained tight lipped about what he knew until his trial. Unfortunately for William, Ted knew this as well. Ted also knew that he was the only man that had anything on him and therefore was the only one that could do any harm to himself or his business. This left little question as to what it was worth to the billionaire to get rid of the man. Gabriel had wiretapped Ted's phones as well as William's, he always did to gain the insider information he needed. On the first day of getting intel, what did Ted do? He called William and advised him that he was going to kill him; he promised the CPA he would be dead by his hand or the hand of a professional. The FBI poured into the man's home, scooped him up, and took him into protective custody.

Gabriel cursed Ted Nulty, again, for how things had played out… just because he couldn't keep his mouth shut for a few weeks. No, he needed to put the fear of God in the mark. Gabriel, of course, because of this blatant disrespect was now staring through a riflescope, seeing a plethora of blood painting the once beautiful building. Agents were lying dead and he saw something he didn't see very often: a dead man whose face had been blown off and smoke from his cigarette finally finding its way back out of the body.

Gabriel was very well aware that time was of the utmost importance. He would waste no more of it worrying about the men on the other side and if any were reporting his shooter's nest location. He pushed up to his knees and crouched over his rifle. Gabriel broke it back down to its original four pieces. He had practiced this act so many times, he could do it in his sleep. The muscle memory took over and he sat back, watching everything work. Gabriel smiled at the speed with which he worked when put in a life and death situation such as this. If he didn't leave, he was no longer going to have a life. He rearranged everything quickly in the toolbox. He had a voice in the back of his head, motivating him to move at the fastest speed he could—the voice screaming, *If you do not get out of here, you are going to be shot. If you do not get out of here, they are going to catch you, torture you, and peel your skin back until you finally die.*

Gabriel slammed the toolbox shut and rose, walking quickly to the door. From his pocket, he pulled a pair of electrician wire cutters and snipped off the zip tie he had placed around the door to keep it from opening. He opened it slowly, looking left and right, surveying the hall and making sure that it was clear. When he saw the coast was clear, he sprinted through the hallway and across to the stairwell. He shut the door as quietly as he could and looked over the railing; he saw two security guards coming up the stairwell. Both men were speaking into radios as they made their way up the steep stairs. He could hear the bigger of the two guards say clearly, "We have someone in the stairwell, Pete, we'll detain him."

He knew if they were wanting to detain him, they would be cautious with him. He had been taking the stairs two at a time, knowing the quicker he left, the better, but at this new development, he slowed it down. When he came around the corner of a set, he decided it would be good enough to play it stupid. He poured his Russian accent back on, yelling frantically and pointing up the stairwell. "I heard gunshots, why the hell did I hear guns? This is hotel, no?"

This calmed the two guards; the younger guard said, "We're looking for any suspicious persons of interest. The police should be here soon. They will secure the building and question guests and help us get everything buckled down."

Gabriel played the part for everything he had… an Oscar-worthy performance. He kept up a heavy breathing and rubbed his dirty hands through his hair. The older guard motioned to the younger and said, "Take him down to the lobby, will you? I'm going to finish the stairs and take the elevator back down. My old knees can't handle this shit anymore."

The kid nodded, and with a nervous smile, pointed to follow him back down the long descent. As they made it down flight after flight of steps, Gabriel knew he was using precious minutes he didn't have to waste. The kid asked, "So, what's wrong with the elevator?"

Gabriel didn't answer and after a minute he asked, "Hey, is this going to be quick. I have to do three more jobs before I go home tonight. My ass boss won't ever pay out overtime for me."

The guard slowed down, turning around with one hand on the railing to say something about following procedures when Gabriel snapped a size-twelve boot directly into the man's chin, snapping his head up and back, propelling him into a backwards arch, down the remainder of the steps. A bloody arch trailed into his descent, landing on him as he hit hard on the floor below. The man's leg entangled in the railing, and as his head cracked the concrete, his bone

94

protruded from his leg below the knee. Blood pooled around his skull and he began to spasm.

Gabriel, again, knew the man had done nothing wrong, but it was either him or the guard. He ran down the rest of the stairs jumping over him and the pool of blood. He reached down, grabbing the guard's radio, and looked at his nametag, which indicated his name was John. Gabriel hit the talk button and said, "Hey, it's John. I am up on ten. I fell and broke my leg in the stairwell. Get up here in the elevator and get me some help."

A voice came back over that might help Gabriel feel a bit less evil. "You stay put, kid. We'll send someone up just as quickly as we can."

Gabriel secured the radio to the inside of his harness and attached an earphone to it, securing it on his own so that he could keep up with the radio chatter that was sure to be plentiful. He turned the volume up and could hear men and women's voices chattering back and forth, unsure what to do about something this high level.

Gabriel raced down the remaining steps that led to the back door, where his van would be waiting for him. He opened it slowly and looked at the room he came through. The kitchen had been emptied; no food was sizzling any longer. The hustle and bustle of the area was now gone. He noticed the only man left in the area was the young guard who had let him in earlier when he arrived, and a new man helping him secure it.

Gabriel pushed through the door, walking towards the young man as if nothing at all was wrong. The two men noticed him approaching and immediately reached for their sides. The first man pulled a Taser—nothing that would kill Gabriel, but with enough volts to put him on his back, killing any chance of him leaving... at least when he wanted to.

Gabriel set the toolbox down slowly, looking nervous. He said, "What is problem? Where everyone go... buddy?"

The guard he didn't know motioned for him to follow them. "Please come with us, sir. We need to speak to everyone. We're assembling guests and workers in the front lobby. We'll try to not detain you for any longer than we need to."

Gabriel looked flustered, rubbing his hand in his hair and shaking his head. He reached behind his head and down into the back of his overalls, pulling a nine-millimeter pistol from a holster attached inside the top of his overalls. The two men's eyes both got wide and the threat of the gun was enough to persuade them to walk backwards, stumbling over each other. Gabriel motioned for them to head towards the cooler and pulled it open as they entered. Both were rewarded with a pistol whip to the back of the head.

Gabriel ran back to the counter, grabbing his toolbox and went through the back doors. He wasn't lucky enough to avoid people. It was just that the people in the hotel were so busy, there was less security staff to have to deal with. He pushed out the door he'd come through, not rushing, but not waiting around to see who was looking for people to question. He quickly noticed two men dressed in identical black suits with bulges underneath their armpits walking around the outside of the back parking lot.

Gabriel thought for a second about trying to make a break for it, but they saw him the moment he had exited the rear delivery door. They knew he shouldn't be outside and wasted no time coming straight for him. They were spread out and coming in slow, training their weapons on his chest.

Gabriel saw this and screamed, "Whoa, guys, settle down, alright? What's going on here? Who are you? Quit pointing those damn things at me. I've had enough gun pointed at me in Russia. I thought in your U S of A you did not do thing like this."

The agent ignored his chatter, yelling across to his partner, "I got this! You go check out the toolbox and see what's inside it." He then spoke directly to Gabriel, "You put that toolbox down now. Do it slowly or I'll blow your ass away."

The other agent walked slowly towards Gabriel, reached up, grabbed the toolbox, and yelled, "Just looks like a lot of..."

That was when he pulled out the top tray, exposing the hand-molded carrying case for Gabriel's favorite weapon. The one-inch thick barrel glistened in the sun. The agent looked over his shoulder as worry and fear spread across his face. "Get cuffs on him. Do it now—he's the guy; he is the fucking guy."

The man approached, never wavering his aim on Gabriel's skull. He spun Gabriel around and slammed him hard against the rusty van. The man yelled with authority, "Get your hands up behind your head now!" To emphasize this, he pulled Gabriel an inch back by his collar and slammed him again into the van's side. He kicked his feet apart like a pro.

Gabriel complied and within a second, his partner was back on his feet and both were standing behind Gabriel. He spoke into his wrist again and said, "We've got a suspect subdued." The man poked Gabriel in the back with his pistol screaming, "Get your hands behind your head! Now, I said!"

He didn't want anyone to get jumpy and shoot him in the back of his head so he complied. Gabriel heard the rattling of handcuffs, and he pushed his wrists against the back of his skull hard and then lifted them back off. The spring under each sleeve brought out two small automatic handguns that Gabriel's open and eager hands were waiting to clutch. The moment they entered his hands, Gabriel pulled the triggers. Each man screamed in pain, which Gabriel could barely hear after firing shots that close to his ears. Gabriel turned and put two more shots in each of the downed agents' heads. Their bodies each jerked in spasms as the final bursts of life exited their bodies, their souls soon to follow.

Gabriel looked at the van and knew that after that stunt there would be no way he'd be getting out of the parking lot. The very fact that men had come from the side of the building probably meant they were securing the obvious exit points first and then moving on to the harder-to-secure spots. He grabbed the toolbox and tossed it into the back, hoping it would char well. He cringed a moment, thinking of how many great shots he'd taken with it and how much he would miss that rifle and its guaranteed reliability.

Gabriel quickly unbuttoned the filthy overalls, glad that he made it a strict habit to always dress in layers, regardless of the temperature. He tore at the buttons once he got past the halfway point, not worried about them being used again. He crumpled them up, tossing them into the back of his van, but not before cutting the leg of the pants off. Gabriel was left wearing a zip up hoodie, blue jeans, and a black shirt. He couldn't have looked any less attention getting… as long as kept the arsenal beneath it hidden from sight.

Gabriel unscrewed the gas cap, quickly forcing the torn pant leg down the hole as far as he could. He put the van in neutral, which was still idling all of this time and let it start rolling down the slight incline, aiming it directly at the side entrance. It was the only way that to get to the rear of the building. Gabriel walked beside it as it picked up momentum and flicked a zippo, lighting the greasy pant leg on fire. He watched the fire for a moment, making sure it was really on fire and wasn't going to go out in twenty feet. When he was confident, he turned and sprinted for the back wall, knowing the gunshots would bring the rest of the agents like flies on shit.

He jumped up the six-foot brick wall and disappeared over its edge. The hotel kept their parking lot separate from the chain restaurants with the wall. Gabriel could see, as he was going over, that there were a chain of black SUVs coming down the path and the old rusty van was making its way slowly but surely towards them. He shrugged, thinking their day was probably going as good as his, but he thought of the positive: unlike them, there was a very strong chance that he would live at least.

Two unlucky men hopped out from the back seats of the government SUV and ran up to the van with their pistols pulled and screaming at the empty van to stop and get out. Since empty vans aren't scared of FBI agents, it kept moving in their direction which happened to be right dead ahead for them.

Gabriel knew how intelligent agents had to be to pass the entrance exams for the academy for the FBI because he'd taken them when weighing his options, as well and had passed them with flying colors. He knew that at Quantico, they were pushed to their limits to be sure they knew everything they should before they are thrown out into the field. Gabriel thought about how his tax dollars were being horribly wasted until he remembered he did not know the last time that he actually had to pay them, as ghosts didn't pay taxes. He watched, wanting to know what happened, and if anyone was going to be on his ass right away. He was baffled that neither man was aware or responding to the fact that a pant leg was hanging from the side of a shitty old van that was on fire.

Gabriel watched the flame disappear inside the van just a moment before it blew up. The van flipped into the air, landing on its top. The two men who seemed a little slow about the van prior were now very much aware that there had been something seriously wrong with the van. The blast knocked them both back off their feet, and black smoke rolled up into the air in waves. The outline of it was drastic against the bright blue sky. The entrance was blocked and the van was too hot to try to pass, leaving him much less to worry about as far as being followed. When he heard the blades of a helicopter, he ran from the scene before it was overhead.

He walked briskly for a few blocks, not looking over his shoulder or coming off as nervous. He knew it took just one cop that thought he looked out of place, after a high-profile hit, to ruin his entire day. Gabriel made it three blocks before coming to a gas station, watching and waiting, when a man in a truck pulled up. Gabriel had been patiently waiting for an older vehicle that probably didn't have a GPS system. He waited for the man to get out and head into the store. Once Gabriel saw that he was out of sight, he walked up to the idling truck, slid in, and left, heading towards safety many miles away.

Gabriel drove to the edge of town and dumped the truck. He put five hundred dollars in the glove box and left the truck locked after wiping it down. He walked the two miles back to his shop where he could shower, get fresh clothes, and pick up his own vehicle. Gabriel made it back in a short time and went through the normal procedure of getting the door unlocked and then disarming the long line of bombs. He went to the back, checking everything as he usually did, and pulled his laptop from the office and fired it up. He sat patiently checking the news and seeing what he had expected to see. They said that there was a manhunt underway and that the FBI was searching feverishly for a lone gunman that may or may not be terrorist related. They described him as wearing dark overalls, armed, and having a hat; he was also white with dark brown hair. Gabriel clicked off the browser and smiled. A tall white guy with brown hair; he felt that he was going to be just fine.

Gabriel opened up his secure site that kept a list of his banking institutions. He was going to transfer some of the huge payment he had received. He didn't think it wise to keep all of his eggs in one basket. He wasn't worried that the rich man was good for it, but sometimes he knew people had bad habits of thinking that once the job was done, so was their need to pay people for their services. This wasn't something that had happened to Gabriel more than once. Gabriel leaned back in his seat thinking of his first few months as a contract killer and remembering one of the first issues that had come up as a hitter.

*****

Shortly after leaving the CIA

He was in his late twenties at the time and had just returned from a large job, where he had taken out a man's business partner who thought he was embezzling. Forsyth, his handler, had just dropped him off a state away and told him to stay off the radar. He sat on a piece-of-shit Greyhound for two days. He remembered the ride very well because it was the last time he had ever ridden on one. He made it home, ready to sleep for a week after being up for what felt like two weeks straight.

He remembered going into his small flat that he was renting for cash from an old lady. He liked her because he knew that she wouldn't report his payments on her taxes, so it was as if he didn't exist. It was a perfect relationship between the two. He had been on a short allowance that Forsyth had loaned him while they had gotten the first of what would be many jobs arranged between the two. Gabriel logged into the bank accounts that Forsyth had helped him set up under fake names. When he logged in, Gabriel had hoped to see six figures in the account. Instead, what he saw was exactly the same amount that was there when he went out of town, a few weeks prior, to finish the job. He had Forsyth on speed dial, and was trying to calm himself before placing the call that would make the rest of his career a thing of legends.

Gabriel hit the button for Forsyth and sat back, waiting. On the fifth ring, he picked up his satellite phone, which was the only way that he ever contacted him. "What's up, kid? I figured I wouldn't hear from you for at least a month. You ready for another job already?"

Forsyth didn't pick up on his sarcasm when he replied, "Yeah, you know, I don't think that I have a choice, but to be ready to work, now do I?"

"Well, you can take all the time you want between jobs, you know. With the kind of money that we are making doing this shit… hell, you can do two or three jobs a year and still retire a rich man ten years from now."

"Well, it'd be hard to live off of what I'm making."

"Jesus! Are you getting greedy already, kid? I wouldn't take so much if you knew how to fly. It's a damn big convenience having a full time pilot at your disposal who can also set up these type of special working assignments."

"So, you're saying that we are making enough money off of these jobs? I guess maybe we should try to get paid more for some of these jobs going forward."

There was nothing but silence on the other end of the line. It took a moment, but eventually the bells and whistles had gone off in his head, and Forsyth said, "He didn't pay us, did he? Damn it! I can't believe that fucker stiffed us! I tell you what; let me get another job lined up for you. We can do something quick and easy. I'll make sure that we get paid in advance this time, I promise. How does that sound? You okay with that?"

"So, we spend over a month researching, and then I waste another two weeks going out on the hit, and in the end, I'm still broke? You're saying that we just write this job off and then you and I start all over again?"

"Yeah, pretty much. You can't go after the hirer. It's against the rules of being a hit man. You are aware of that, right? I know it sounds stupid, but if you go around killing the people that hire you, you're going to get into some serious shit in the industry, and you are going to do it very quickly."

"Well, the only reason that I'm going after that motherfucker is because he stiffed us. He stiffed me, and I can't live off of nothing. I'm sure as hell not going to just walk away. If they don't want me to come after them, then maybe they ought to have fucking paid me. I don't give a shit who he is. There is nothing that will keep him safe from me. I mean, he was aware of what I do for a living, so he is either incredibly well protected or completely stupid! Either way, there isn't any amount of luck that's going to keep his ass safe from me!"

"I don't think it's a good idea," Forsyth said.

"I need you to give me his name and address, and I will take care of the rest."

"I can't do that, slick. It's bad business. I'm telling you, take the loss, and let it go."

"Fine."

"Fine... wait, you mean you're going to listen to me? You're going to let things go and we just move on, G? Oh shit, you had me worried. Fuck, you know what? I'm going to go make a damn drink. I say you do the same; maybe have four or five and then we'll talk about a brand new day tomorrow."

"Yeah, I'm okay with it. I just need you to wire the money that I would have gotten from doing this job out of your account and stick it in mine."

"Stick it in your ass—*that*'s what I'm going to do! You've lost your fucking mind!"

"Oh, I'm thinking very damn clearly, Forsyth; you get me my money or you give me his address. One way or another, I'm going to get paid for this job, and I'm going to get it fucking soon. What's it going to be boss? You're the handler, you set up the job, you get the money, and you pay me. If you are just setting up jobs and not getting me paid, I'm kind of confused. What the hell am I doing keeping you around? You aren't trying to set yourself up for your own personal hit, right? I mean, you don't have a death wish that I don't know about, do you? Are you suicidal?"

"I don't have that kind of money. Christ! You know how much I spend on women and booze. Hell, it's not a cheap lifestyle. Being the man that I am, it's actually pretty damn difficult. To answer your other question, I plan to live out every last waking minute on this earth that baby Jesus will allow me to."

"So, then you give me the address; I'll go there and collect the money. Hell, I'll even give you the money that you should have earned this time. I say 'this time' only because next time I do a job, you're going to make damn sure that I get paid before I ever pull the trigger. I am not kidding! I want the money and I want it before I go. We don't do a job until we have been paid at least half up front."

"Deal, I'll email you his name and address once I get home. Take a day and get some sleep; it'll do you good. If you change your mind... you know, about that whole murdering the guy that hired you thing, you let me know."

"I tell you what. If you don't hear from me in the next ten minutes, just assume I still want to cut his head off."

"You know, I think that you might be taking this a little far. Don't you?"

"I think that regardless of how this plays out, you're going to get a lot of business, and that you're also going to make a lot of money. You also aren't ever going to get stiffed for a job or have someone think twice about doing so. The reason people screw over handlers is because you all think that those people hiring us are too powerful to do something. Well, you know what? Those days are over. If they want to make it through another day, they won't fuck with us. They sure as hell won't fuck with me!"

"You know something, kid?"

"What?"

"You scare the shit out of me. You let me know if I ever piss you off, alright?"

"Why's that?"

"Because I'll do my very best to make sure I apologize to you in the most sincere of ways that I can. You aren't really going to cut his head off, are you?"

"If you want to stay on my good side, you make damn sure that when I get up in the morning, I have what I need. I don't have expensive tastes like you, but I'm not doing this shit for free. I wouldn't do anything that crazy."

"Hey, man, you'll have it in the morning, on my life."

"You sure that's how you want to say it?"

"It'll be there, I promise."

Gabriel hung up the phone, laid out the gear that he knew he would need to travel cross-country to wherever the man was located, and slept like the dead. When he awoke, as promised, the name of the hirer was sitting encrypted in his email. The two didn't trust people or hackers on the web, and they shared an email account. They input the message that they wanted the other to see, and they saved it as a draft, never actually sending the message. Between the two of them, it only took a quick phone call to let the other know there was a message waiting. He read the email and was off to California a day later, rested and still very much wanting his funds paid.

Gabriel had tried to call the man in order to collect and give him a chance to pay. He had thought about how worried Forsyth was about their reputation and felt if he could avoid unnecessary killing, it would be the smart play. "Hello, I'd like to speak to Dr. David McBroom, please. It's about a financial matter."

A few minutes later, the man came on the line already acting as if he was being disrupted. "This is Dr. David McBroom. I'm very busy and I don't have time to talk bills with someone. Why can't you people ever call the damn accountants like you're supposed to do? You know, if you'd have gone to college, you might not have to do jobs like these."

Gabriel waited for the man to quit his rant and shut up before he continued, "I don't think your accountant handles this type of thing, sir."

"Get to the point, kid. I've got patients that I need to see, and my deadbeat partner hasn't been in all damn week. You wouldn't believe how useless they are; they're probably worse than having a damn wife."

"It's going to be a long time before he comes in, don't you think?"

"What are you talking about? He'll be in eventually. He always comes in. This place is his dream. Look, call my accountant and have him pay you; it will be no problem. Good day to..."

Gabriel was past patience and already disliked this man more after one minute on the phone than he had when he just thought he was going to stiff him on his bill. "Your partner won't be in because he's dead. He's dead because I killed him. I'm calling you because you were the absolute dumb fuck who told me, or told my handler who arranges things for me, that you would pay us a prearranged amount of money to kill him for you."

"And you are calling for what?"

"Please tell me you aren't that dense. Are you?"

"Well, let me ask you this; As far as I know, the way life works is, once you take it you aren't able to bring back the dead, are you?"

"No, no I can't. But I can add to it. By the time I'm done, I can make you wish that I wouldn't have taken my time."

"Don't threaten me, kid. I've been around too long and have dealt with too much shit. The likes of you calling and hounding me for money is going to do absolutely nothing to move along any process of trying to extort money from me."

"It isn't extortion when you owe it to someone. I'm not worried about collecting it because I'll get my money; I promise you this. I can also promise you that if you see my face, it'll be the last thing you ever see. If you don't understand that, then let me dumb it up for you. If you don't pay me, if you don't make an arrangement right now with me, then you're dead."

"Kid, if you knew what kind of security I keep at the house and around me, you'd never have even made this call. I think that you need to reassess your loss, here, and move on."

"That's your final word then?"

The man hung up on Gabriel and Gabriel headed to California. Dr. McBroom didn't appreciate that when he sought out a man to kill his partner, he had gotten the best, and got exactly what he should have paid for.

Two days later, when the doctor came home, he had instantly wished, with every bit of his soul, that he had paid the stranger on the phone. He wished he'd paid them whatever they wanted to be paid. The man walked into his entryway and saw how empty it was. When he walked into the living room, he dropped his briefcase where he stood. He stared in shock, looking at the scene before him. His bottom lip quivered, unable to speak at first. The room was filled with his bodyguards—his dead bodyguards—all lined up against the wall.

Each of them had their pistols lying empty on their legs. Gabriel was sitting in front of them in a chair and holding a silenced pistol. When the doctor turned to run, Gabriel put a bullet through each of the man's kneecaps. The man screamed in agony for anyone, anyone at all, to come and save him. He collapsed onto the ground, writhing in pain. He pushed up, trying to drag himself away and gave up very quickly, the pain too much to handle.

Gabriel never even stood up. He watched the man squirming on the ground; his face was red and tears poured from his eyes. Gabriel kept the pistol pointed at the man's temple. "I need you to stop moving, David. If you move, I shoot you. Do you understand? There is no question in my mind of what I will do to you if you make any rash and stupid movements."

Gabriel stood and walked up to him. He used the barrel of the gun to open the man's sport coat, making sure he was not invoking his right to the second amendment. The man, who wouldn't stop screaming, finally yelled, "My other bodyguards aren't going to show you mercy, do you know that? You should leave now if you want to have the slightest chance of living!"

Gabriel stared the man in the face. He turned around, counting the number of guards behind him and said, "Wait— do you mean that you have more bodyguards than this at your home that you employ?"

The man laughed hysterically, hope flooding through his veins, "Yes, those are my real guards. They are going to torture you until you only *think* you understand the meaning of the word *pain*."

Gabriel looked at him, a knowing smile on his face as he finished patting him down. "I killed them first. They're downstairs in their makeshift poker room. I hope you weren't paying them much, because it's been more difficult sneaking into homes in a third world country than it was here. I think you were wasting your money."

The man looked up with steel in his eyes. "You aren't going to last long, you know, if the two of you are going to be going after people who hire you, right? I mean, what does that say about you?"

Gabriel stood back up, looking around at the men on the ground, and put a foot back and kicked a steel-toed boot into the man's gut. "It says that I want to get paid. It means if I am not paid, you don't live."

Gabriel pulled out a small laptop, placing it in front of the man. "Pay me now; I want twenty percent more for my trouble. If you come after me, if you even think about me, talk about me, you'll be a dead man. I can promise you that."

The doctor screamed in pain as Gabriel sat there patiently, waiting for him to punch in the numbers. He yelled, "I need a hospital… I won't give you your money until I get medical treatment!"

"Aren't you a doctor? Take care of yourself once I leave."

The man stripped his coat off, ripped the thousand-dollar suit into pieces, and wrapped each of his knees tightly, screaming as he applied the makeshift bandages. He yelled, "Now take me to a hospital!"

Gabriel's patience was done; he was now more worried about getting paid than the man's long-term health. He put the computer on the man's lap and pointed at it. "You need to pay me now, or you're going to have more bullet wounds that need to be healed."

The doctor shook his hands free of the blood, wiping them on his ruined pants; he punched in the numbers and handed it back to Gabriel, who confirmed it. Gabriel closed the laptop and started walking towards the man. He pulled a knife from behind his back, gripping it tight. The doctor freaked when he saw this and started screaming for his life. "But I paid you, I paid you! What are you doing, I don't understand!"

"You remember when I called you? What I said? That if I needed to come collect, you were going to die? Well, unfortunately for you, you've seen my face. You shouldn't have seen my face, which wouldn't have happened if you had paid my handler when you asked us to do something for you. You see, now I have to make an example out of you."

"But what does that mean? I don't understand."

Gabriel gripped the man's hair, tilting his head back. The man gripped at Gabriel's arms, trying a last-ditch effort to survive, which did not surprise Gabriel. Gabriel took the butt end of the knife and smashed it into the man's nose four times until his nose shattered and blood poured down his face. His crisp, white dress shirt was a mess of blood and snot. He gripped his face, still yelling, as Gabriel ran the knife across his neck, slicing through the many layers of skin. He didn't stop until all that held it on was a small flap of skin. He left him lying there, in front of his bodyguards, his head hanging on by a miracle.

Gabriel ripped the man's shirt open and carved a dollar sign into his flabby chest. He pulled out a digital camera that had data web synced to it. He called Forsyth as he walked out of the house. "Hey! You sitting at your computer by chance?"

"Maybe, why... I thought you were on some holy crusade to go out and try to get some of our money paid back to us."

"Check your bank account and see if there is anything there that will make your day a little more pleasant."

Forsyth typed slowly, a little bit nervous about what he was going to see; when he hit enter, he saw the numbers stacked up in his offshore account. "Do I want to ask what you did to get that money?"

Gabriel hit send on the camera. "Check out saved drafts on our account... see if you think that might help out with the future of payments."

Forsyth stared at the images, completely shocked. "Holy shit! I've heard the stories, but Jesus Christ, did you really have to cut the man's head off?"

"Yeah, I did. I don't want this to be a repeat situation. If you can't collect with this, then the two of us are going to have to have one serious 'come to Jesus' meeting. I hope that you understand that is not a conversation that you're going to want to have."

"No. I don't think we're going to have to do anything like that. But tell me, because I'm dying to know if you're just fucking with me... did you just Photoshop that? I mean it would be genius, but people could look up something like that. I know you're smart enough to know that, right? I mean if these pics are just you dicking with people."

"Forsyth, if you haven't figured out that I'm lacking in the personality department, then let me be the first to advise you that I have no personality when it comes to money. I never have and never will use it in a joking matter, and I'm never going to get stiffed again. If you want to make sure that I'm not full of shit, I would say that you could simply check the *California Daily News*. I'm pretty confident that there is a good chance that they won't miss out on putting in such a juicy story."

"So, you think the cops are going to find them before the next edition of the paper comes out?"

"They'd have to be really big assholes if they didn't, since I already called them and advised where they are and what happened."

"You called the cops on yourself?"

"Yep, and I'm leaving now. I'd hate to try and talk this out with the police force; I don't know if they could handle having to deal with a guy like me. Their psych department would be trying their damnedest to figure out what's wrong with me after they see the dollar symbol carved into his chest."

Forsyth scrolled through the rest of the pictures and looked at the dollar amount in a second window. "You might have sent me too much money, you realize that right?"

Gabriel was walking down the street, keeping an eye over his shoulder, and saw that the street couldn't have been clearer. "Yes, we got a twenty percent bonus for having to wait for the money. It seems a couple bullets to the knee were enough to motivate him to pay the interest. I need to get off the line; you get the next job lined up and let me know when it's ready. Don't come with excuses about not being paid. Those pictures and the newspaper ought to be more than enough to never have to deal with stupid shit like this again. We're professionals; remember that. We aren't first-time hitters."

Forsyth just stared at the money and the pictures. "No we aren't going to have any more trouble, kid. Why don't you take a week off and I'll do my best to get you some work lined up if you're ready to go?"

"Get it arranged I'm ready to go. You line them up I'll take them out. I don't need breaks."

"Don't burn yourself out kid. You might not like what you become."

"Look if you knew how many hits I've done the last five years for the CIA, you might not be so worried about what I'm going to become. You got any other fatherly advice?"

"Yeah go get laid kid. You are too damn uptight." Forsyth hit the phone's end button and sat back stretching and putting his hands behind his head. He smiled, realizing that cash cow wasn't even the appropriate thing to call his killer for hire. He couldn't have been happier thinking of the fact that he didn't need to worry about future shortcomings with people trying to rip the two of them off. He logged into the job site and started searching for his next contract.

*****

Present day

Gabriel was unworried about them finding him. He had an inner knowledge of how the FBI worked and the way they approached their jobs. He locked up his place and sat back in his truck, ready to write the day off as a partial success and glad that he hadn't gotten caught. The idea of taking a capsule that would make his brain hemorrhage until he died was not a pleasant thought. He always kept something in his pocket just in case the worst happened. He pulled out of his space slowly, looking around and making sure nothing looked out of place. He had a few drunks that were staples in the neighborhood, and if they weren't around, he knew it meant they were dead or there was something wrong going on. He made a habit out of dropping off a couple bottles of whiskey a month anytime that he was around.

He was trying to relax when his phone started to buzz. He ignored it and let it go to voicemail. He knew no one had this number so automatically wrote it off as a wrong number. When it rang a second and then a third time, he started to look in his rear view mirror a bit more suspiciously. On the fourth ring, he hit the button to speak. He waited, not saying anything. He wanted to know who it was, but if they didn't say anything, he was going to end the call. He had no patience for games. After a minute, a voice came over the line, "Hello?"

Gabriel rolled his eyes, thinking there was a strong chance that his day, which was already not going great, was going to go completely to hell in a handbag. "Yes, do you have the right phone number?"

The voice came back instantly, this time trying to sound a little more confident. "Well, you tell me, son. Is this Gabriel that I am speaking with?"

"I hope you planned on what you were thinking when you made this call. You could be making the worst decision you ever have before."

"Gabriel, it's Tony… Tony Baker. We need to talk, son."

"Tony Baker… what the fuck are you doing calling me?"

"It's about a job we have that we..."

"Stick your job where I'll stick my foot if I see you or anyone coming after me! You don't remember when you guys thought that it was a good idea to try and bring me in to offer me some work? How many people did you lose that time? Did you think that I'd changed my mind over time, Baker?"

"Uh, well yeah, I was hoping that we might be able to offer you enough to get you to come do some contract work for us?"

"You don't have enough spooks sitting around anymore, looking for something to do, that you can't get the job taken care of on your own?"

"Well, not counting the number of men that you sent back to us in pieces, we've had a few different Presidents since then, if you haven't been keeping up with the times. Unfortunately, neither of them was very keen on the idea of secret operations, so our entire budget has been screwed, son."

"I don't see how this is my problem. You remember the last time we spoke and I mentioned I was out, right? Did you think I was kidding? I'm sure you are staring at my file right now and can see my history of evaluations. Does it mention anywhere about me having a personality?"

"No, it doesn't, but we've been ordered to take care of a threat and if you don't help, you might as well write yourself off for dead too."

"I'm not an easy kill, Baker."

"No. You are quite the pain in the ass, actually. You see, what is happening is top secret and I can't really disclose details to you until you..."

"Don't do me any favors, boss. I don't need any jobs, I don't need CIA money, and I don't want to work for you guys ever again. I hope that you can understand I've been fucked over too many times to go back."

A second voice came on the line, cutting Gabriel off. "Sorry, son, we don't have time for shit like this. This is Frank Fox. I'm in charge of Tony and I apologize for having to take this harsh tone with you, but we are on a timetable. We need your expertise for a short time. It'll be your biggest payday ever. Hell, it'll be like we are paying you with your own money."

Gabriel did not like the way that came off and slammed on his brakes, pulling over on the side of the street. He ripped out his laptop, feeling his blood pressure rising as he waited for the yellow biohazard to flash again. When it did, he punched the keys and brought up his accounts, showing four of the nine banks that he used regularly. When they came up on his screen, it showed a current balance for each one. All of them showed one cent available. Gabriel didn't feel sick because he knew that he could get the money back, but he was confident that whoever this Frank guy was, he had a short life span left if he had anything to do with his money going missing.

Gabriel put the vehicle back in gear and pulled away from the curb. He pulled a silenced pistol from his coat and set it on the armrest next to him, never letting go. He wasn't going to waste time if he needed it. He wanted to be a second ahead of them. "Tony, I think that you and your friend have got a death wish. Did you know that he'd taken my money?"

Tony hit the mute button. "Jesus Christ, Frank! Are you absolutely bat shit crazy? I don't know about you, but once I can retire, I'd like to do that and I'd also like the ability to sleep at night. You are underestimating him. He's going to come here if you don't fix this!"

"We are in a secure, armed building filled with armed men. We are going to be fine. He's going to change his mind. It's Handler 101, for god sakes. You took the classes."

"Yes I did—a million years ago, and ever since taking them, I've never met anyone like the man you are currently screwing over. If you think that these men are going to intimidate Gabriel, you're fucking crazy. He'll come in, slit their throats, and do it with a smile on his face."

"He isn't a ghost, Baker; he's just a man. I'm well aware of how dangerous he is. I just don't think you understand how badly we need him."

"Oh, I understand how dangerous the situation at hand is, but I think you might be trading one evil for another. I think you're going to be getting more than you bargained for and unfortunately, you're dragging me into the shit right with you. The only problem is, I seem to be the only one who cares that we are pissing the devil off."

"Just relax. You'll get to retire and you'll get to sleep at night. I thought you needed to have a pair hanging between your legs to be a handler."

Baker sat back, picked up his pack of smokes, and smiled, motioning for Frank to introduce himself to the man. Frank adjusted his collar, smiling, and hit the mute key on the phone. "Son, this is Frank Fox, I'm Tony's boss. We need you to do a job for us. Tony was unaware that I had taken your money and he seems very nervous of the personal opinion that you carry of him. Your reputation seems to follow you even into CIA retirement."

"So, you were the one that took my money, thinking that if you had my bankroll, you'd be able to get this set up?"

Frank laughed, which left Gabriel white knuckling the steering wheel. "You want to know something funny, son?"

"Fox, you just don't get the point."

"You know that we were the ones who hired you for the job on the FBI building? We owed a huge favor for some help that Nulty gave us. When his man got picked up, ready to narc and expose secrets, which would eventually make their way back to us, we went ahead and made some arrangements. We needed to get you in town and having you here for a job with a big payday seemed like the best idea. We wanted to make sure that you were still the man for the job. Unfortunately, things don't always go as planned, but we were very happy with how everything worked out for you."

"You hired me so that you could get my access to my accounts and then you hired someone to trace and hack and steal my money. I'm going to kill you; I hope you understand that. It's going to hurt and it's a promise, it isn't a 'maybe'. It's just a when and how bad it will hurt, you cocky fuck."

"Just take a look at a file we have. You do a quick job and you get your money back. There is no reason to take any of this personally."

Tony whispered, "He takes everything personally you, dumbshit."

"Don't forget who you are talking to, Baker. I'm your boss! You treat me with a little damn respect."

"Oh, I know who I'm talking to… a dead man sums it up pretty good."

Frank said, "So, can I send you the file to have you take a look?"

The line was silent; Gabriel didn't reply. He hit the end button on his call and plugged in his cell phone, tracking the call with software that the CIA might not even have at their disposal. Within a minute, he was driving back to his warehouse, where he exchanged his job harness and vest for hell's fury that had more deadly weapons than a metal detector could handle.

Chapter 8
Introductions

Gabriel drove past the building, circling it twice at two blocks away; after that, he moved in a block. He saw nothing, which did absolutely nothing to put his fears at ease. He looked around and pulled in quickly to the underground parking garage, driving very fast. When he got to the bottom of the garage, he parked in a dark corner where he wouldn't be approached by anyone quickly. He knew that they were already watching him, but didn't want to make it any easier for them or more difficult for himself.

Gabriel opened the rear passenger door to his SUV. He knew this would require heavier artillery and pistols wouldn't be the best choice. Gabriel was all about keeping as much distance between himself and an unknown number of security people. He grabbed a twelve-gauge, automatic shotgun and slung it over his shoulder and carried a black backpack in his hand. The elevator opened and two men greeted him cautiously, with hands held up. One of the men said, "Mr. Baker and Mr. Fox would like to talk to you. Would you please lay down your weapons and come with us, sir?"

Gabriel smiled. "That's it? I just lay down my guns and you two take me upstairs?"

They stared at each other a moment longer than Gabriel was willing to trust; when one went to open his mouth, Gabriel pulled up the shotgun, firing twice and knocking both of them off of their feet with twelve-gauge slugs. They landed on their backs, writhing in pain and clutching their chests. Gabriel knew they would be wearing bulletproof tactical vests and that if they stayed on the ground, their chances of making it home would be greatly improved.

Not waiting around, Gabriel walked with a purpose and pulled his pistol as he walked by the two men. When he got closer to the elevators, he shot out the cameras that focused on the bank of elevators that took guests up the stairs. When the doors parted, he aimed and took out the one camera that was inside the elevator as well. Gabriel hit the button for the lobby and knelt down inside the elevator, keeping one foot between the heavy steel doors to make sure that he was not going to become an unwilling passenger on the elevator. He set the backpack down carefully and pulled the line on the inside. A red beeping light from the backpack turned on; Gabriel hit the doors' close button, then turned on his heel and sprinted towards the stairwell. Once there, he took three steps at a time. He counted to 30 as he neared the top of the stairs, and then he waited a moment for the perfect time to exit the stairwell.

The security officers of the building lined up outside the elevator with their semi-automatic pistols drawn to subdue the man. They had orders to bring him upstairs, but were not going to get shot in the process. When the elevator's light blinked on the floor, announcing its arrival, the two doors parted. What the guards saw when the doors parted was not what they expected. One of the men walked forward towards it, gun trained as if, somehow, it was going to pull a pistol and shoot him. When he got a bit closer, he heard the beeping in the bag and he looked over his shoulder. "Hey guys, this fucking thing is beeping."

One of the senior guards yelled, "Well, don't stand there! Fucking move, move, move... we got to go!"

All of the men turned and tried to sprint for cover. They made a valiant effort at attempting to put as much distance as they could, but unfortunately for the men, they all failed miserably. When the bag exploded, the blast's force catapulted them into the air. Gabriel opened the stairwell door and sprinted into the lobby, going unnoticed with the plethora of bodies and shrapnel shooting everywhere and the smoke engulfing the floor. Gabriel ran hard to the second set of elevators at the opposite end that went to the top floor offices.

He sat in the elevator, feeling awkward listening to the sounds of Melissa Etheridge that accompanied him to the top. As the elevator rose, he took a few deep breaths and put a pistol in each hand, not knowing for sure what to expect as he waited for the doors to open and possibly leave him in a dangerous position. As the doors opened, Gabriel slid to the side, his back up against the buttons. A hailstorm worth of bullets painted the silver doors a goldish-copper tone. Screams from the outside yelled, "Where the hell is he? Where is he? I thought you said he got on the elevator?"

Gabriel walked out, firing two shots quickly at nothing. He was past the point of worrying if these men went home. They'd sent steel his way and he wasn't about to die because of compassion and the worry for others. The two shots weren't wasted and they weren't a warning. His next five shots were all center mass, knocking all of the men dressed in black suits on their asses. The ones who were smart enough to wear a bulletproof vest would still be around to see tomorrow. Gabriel walked past them quickly; any that tried standing got a reason to get new dental work.

He ran forwards in the empty hallway, now all alone. As he ran past an open space, a leg came up, kicking both of his hands into the air. The force with which they slammed into his arms was enough to make him lose both pistols and they slid away from him.

A hand the size of a bowling ball reached out gripping Gabriel by the neck, lifting him effortlessly off of the ground. Gabriel clawed at the man's wrists, punching them and hitting, trying to free himself. Gabriel was choking, and he knew it from the lack of oxygen that was getting to his brain. His eyes started to roll into the back of his head when the man made his mistake, the only one he would make, but it was enough to set up Gabriel to have a chance. The man used his oversized muscles and launched Gabriel into the air. He hit hard on the marble floor, sliding back ten feet until a wall stopped his path, crashing into it head first.

Gabriel sat for just a second assessing his situation and body; he didn't think he had any broken bones yet. He rolled over, pushing up to his feet and staggering a little as he regained his balance before he let himself fall back to his hands and knees. Gabriel got a good view of the man; he was easily six feet eight inches tall compared to Gabriel's six-foot plus frame.

He had to weigh at least three hundred pounds and he moved with the agility of someone half his size. He made the mistake of underestimating Gabriel as an adversary and assumed that he was going to be an easy target. The man didn't want to let Gabriel rise to his feet, and as Gabriel pushed up on his hands and knees, pretending to get up slowly, the stranger ran at him, winding up a kick to punt Gabriel across the room.

As the man's foot flew up towards his ribs, Gabriel spun to the side, catching his leg and lifting it up as high as he could. As the man wavered in the air, losing his balance, Gabriel pulled down on a handle on his harness, releasing a stiff blade knife from its holster, and plunged the knife into the rear of his thigh.

Gabriel pulled the knife out quickly, and as the man fell to the ground, he stabbed him in the side of the other thigh. The man screamed in agony. Gabriel left the knife in place this time, and as the man's skull smashed to the ground, Gabriel pulled another of his nine-millimeter pistols out and placed it next to the man's temple. Gabriel said, "Let me guess. You're probably the big bad motherfucker most of the time in your role in life. Well, I'm the meanest fucker you've ever met. "

An intercom cracked before he pulled the trigger of the

pistol and a clear, calm voice came over, filling the quiet room. "Gabriel, can you please refrain from killing Alexander? He really is… or I guess should say, *was* quite good. I hope for his sake, he has some backup skills to keep himself useful during his time to recoup."

Gabriel looked up and around, looking for a camera. He saw one focusing in and out towards him. He took the pistol, flipped it in his hand, and pistol-whipped the man repeatedly until he was knocked unconscious. Gabriel said, "I wouldn't want him doing anything stupid."

He stood, patted the man down, removing all of his weapons, and then collected his own pistols he'd lost after encountering the man. He slid them back in their predetermined spots on his harness and rolled his shoulders, feeling better after that throw with every second that passed.

Gabriel walked past the man, looking around and ensuring that no one else wanted to have an outcome like Alexander. He went straight ahead to the end of the rows of oak doors. He didn't knock because the doors opened on their own as he approached them. Gabriel walked in, glancing around the room. A man in a dark gray suit spun the chair around and crossed his legs after pushing up a pair of gold wire-rimmed glasses. He set a red folder, labeled with the word *Classified* on the desk and stared at Gabriel. "You are very good, Gabriel, aren't you? It's a shame you're not a full-time staff employee."

Gabriel stared at the man. "Can I assume that you are Frank? Where the hell is Tony? I would love to see him; is he around?"

Frank shrugged. "Honestly, and don't take any offense, but once you hung up, he was pretty confident you were going to come here and try to kill us. Which, of course, doesn't seem like it was that far of a potshot call, was it?"

Gabriel lifted his pistol, aimed it at the man's face, and said, "I want to know what the fuck you were thinking, taking everything I had. I can understand trying to make a point; I've been there and I've done it before. But when you take everything that a man owns and then threaten that he needs to do what you want if he ever wants his money back… well, it just seems like you have a goddamn death wish. Don't you think, Frank?"

"You're a hard man to get the attention of. I think that, unfortunately, this was going to be the only way that I could tell you any of this. I have more news to tell you, of course, that I think might just give you the motivation that you need to have."

"Talk. This day needs to be over soon or there's going to be a lot more killing taking place, and it's going to start with you and Tony, when I find him."

"There might be more here than you can handle knowing," he said.

"When I started my day, I had every intention of shooting a mark. I accomplished that and then had you to deal with, ruining my entire damn day. What answers do you think you have or things you think you can tell me that will make me want to do anything that you want?"

"You know as well as anyone that we are the sheriff of the world, don't you? There is a terror cell in—"

Gabriel cut him off. "There is always a damn terror cell and there's always a threat to America. What makes these guys different?"

"You're aware of the Chicago Marathon Bombing, right?"

Gabriel walked forward, took a seat, and rested the pistol on the armrest, still pointing straight for Frank's head. "If you know anything about me, you wouldn't need to ask me such ignorant questions, would you?"

"So, you lost your family. What if I told you that the group, Allah's Hand, was responsible for it? Or at least for supplying the idea for it to the two men that set off the main bombs. The bombs that were responsible for taking out your family? Would that make you even the least bit interested?"

Gabriel leaned forward. "You've got my attention."

"We think they have made their way stateside, and we believe that our intel is solid, which I'm sure that you have heard before. I trust that you want revenge and your money back, right? Well, by doing this one job, you will get both. We need you to get back the scientist and we need you to take out their leader, Imad Al-Din. He took over after Hassan died last year. Is that something you think you can do?"

"What's to stop me from blowing your damn head off? You've had me running around for weeks setting up to kill a fucking CPA when you knew that the people who killed my family were in the states and I could have killed them by now? What the hell is wrong with you?"

"We needed to have one hundred percent confirmation before we sent someone like you in. You having to take the man out at the FBI safe house was the only way we saw that would get you here. We were hoping for a smoother transition, but the references in your file show you to being financially motivated. Which wasn't a surprise since you are a contract killer; that was really the shining light. It brought me to the conclusion that we could get you here if we borrow, or let's say, made your money less available for a short time."

"Which means?"

"That, as God is my savior, you will get every cent back once you take care of this."

"God isn't your savior; I will be. You said there was a scientist that needed to be retrieved. What exactly makes this man so important?"

"The doctor specializes in germs and diseases and the modification of them. Twelve months ago, he and his family disappeared. The only family member of his that wasn't taken was his wife."

"What did she have to say when questioned about her husband and family?"

"She didn't have many answers for us, Gabriel."

"Because?"

"Because she had a bullet put through her skull."

"What did they want the scientist for?"

"We think they are modifying different strands of diseases. Once they find the one they think can be a global killer, we think they'll release it to the public."

"So, the people responsible for killing my family are now trying to take out everyone in America? Fuck, what a great day! Do you have any other good news for me?"

"They are holding him in a research facility in the states and, needless to say, it is very well armed. It's going to be a true bitch trying to get into it.

Gabriel said, "If I don't get this stopped, you're still paying me, do you realize this? I want every last fucking cent deposited, and that is non-negotiable at this point. Me getting back my money is the only thing that I'm worried about."

"Yes, I read about what happened to one of your early contracts in California and I'd love to be able to avoid that. But you do realize, if this gets out it's a global killer and money won't matter at that point. It will be a ridiculously small number of people that are immune to the drug."

"It's easier than thinking that I had a part in unleashing death upon America," Gabriel said.

"It isn't your fault if you fail. But we're at a point where our resources have been so diminished that we can't do anything but ask you to do what you do. You can go in guns blazing, do whatever you have to do. Nothing is too much, but there is no backup plan. If you fail, that's it. If they are ready to unleash that hell on the United States, we are all dead."

"I'm in. I'm starting to wish I would've taken that vacation and skipped this job," Gabriel said.

Frank leaned back in his seat and hit the intercom. "Jonathan, could you come in here please. We are ready for you."

A man dressed in a black suit came in and sat down. He looked over to Gabriel, smiled nervously, and said, "My name is Jonathan. What's your name?"

Gabriel stared at the man, and then at Frank. "What the hell is this? I don't do partners. I never have, never will."

Jonathan who had not been properly informed about Gabriel cockily said, "You don't understand I'm the best you've ever seen."

Frank worriedly looked at the two men, realizing he should have had a little more of a conversation with Gabriel before inviting Jonathan in. Gabriel lifted the gun up to the man's head and cocked the hammer. "Do I look like I need a partner?"

Frank intervened, "He isn't really so much a partner. He's a chauffeur of sorts. If you would just read the file a bit more carefully, you will notice that the target is not anywhere close to here and the quickest way to get there is to have a pilot. We assume since you worked with Mr. Forsyth back in the beginning of your career, you aren't capable of flying your own helicopter or airplane, if the opportunity came to light, right? Well, Jonathan is the best pilot we have and he can get you wherever you need to go before it can get worse."

Gabriel lowered the pistol and slid it back in its holster, snapping it into place. He stood and started walking for the door. Frank said, "Wait, I thought you were going to take the assignment. I thought you were going to help."

Gabriel never turned back. He just talked as he walked. "Jonathan, if you're going to fly me somewhere you're going to have to get off your ass to get there. We aren't going to save anyone if we stay here fucking around, are we?"

Frank whispered, "Good luck, Jonathan; try not to piss him off too much, will you? I'd hate to see him upset."

Jonathan grabbed the folder that Gabriel was supposed to have read and ran after the man, which he knew nothing about. He looked down at the folder that had his name on it then looked up. He shook his head, defeated, and said, "Gabriel? Like the angel of fucking death! Are you kidding me?"

He ran to catch up with Gabriel. He got through the door and put a hand on Gabriel's shoulder. The moment he touched him, he knew it was the mistake of the day. Jonathan said, "We need to get a couple of things straight before we do this."

Gabriel spun on his heel, gripping his arm by the elbow and wrist, and then spun him around, smashing him into the wall. His head cracked against the marble wall. Gabriel smashed his forearm into Johnathan's jugular and whispered, "Let's not get confused. If I didn't need to have a lift, then I would be just as happy throwing you off the roof to save the fucking bullet. You don't strike me as the type that would be missed."

He released the pressure and let Jonathan drop to the ground, sitting there with a look of bewilderment on his face. Gabriel continued walking towards the elevator. "Oh, yeah. Don't ever lay another hand on me again."

*****

Frank watched this transpiring from his office over the video monitor feed and shook his head. "I hope this guy is as good as his resume."

Tony slid out of the closet, red faced, as soon as Jonathan had shut the door a couple minutes before. "I don't know what it takes to impress you, Frank, but if Gabriel doesn't have it, you aren't ever going to find it."

"Well, if he fucks it up we're going to have to find a way to spin this so that there's no shit rolling down the hill on us."

"We need to find a way to explain this when he succeeds. We aren't going to have any good excuses for why we hired an assassin who is no longer employed by the CIA."

Frank pointed to the seat across from his desk. "Let's get started, then, either way. I want to have quick answers ready to roll out to whoever is asking."

*****

Gabriel and Jonathan pushed through to the hallway,

taken back for a second at all the medics who were shooting daggers at Gabriel. The men who were conscious couldn't help but stare at the mysterious man. They eyed their pistols as Gabriel passed. Gabriel said, "You touch it and all bets are off."

One of them, knowing it'd most likely be his only chance to ask the stranger something, said, "Who in the hell are you? What makes you such hot shit?"

Gabriel stopped walking and looked at the numerous downed men. He watched the medics working away on their wounds. "The difference between you and me is that I'm not lying on the floor, being tended to like a bitch... and you are."

Gabriel walked backwards the rest of the distance to the elevator. He hit the button with his elbow and waited patiently with his hand gripping his pistol until the silver doors parted and he stepped in. Jonathan went in slowly and stood on the opposite side, trying to regain some composure and get his suit straight again. Gabriel let Jonathan hit the appropriate button to go straight to the top of the large building; the silence between the two men was deafening. Gabriel was a man used to sitting somewhere for days, not saying anything aloud. Jonathan started thinking of different things to say and wasn't sure anything was going to be receptive to Gabriel. Finally, he said, "Want to hear a joke?"

Gabriel smiled and said, "Oh, do I."

"Knock knock." Gabriel stood there silently, so he tried again, "Knock knock." Silence "You do know you're supposed to say 'who's there', right?"

Gabriel was silent then said, "Knock knock."

Jonathan, hopeful, said, "Who's there?"

"Go fuck yourself."

He reached over close to Jonathan, invading his personal space and took the folder. He saw his name on it and ripped it off and slid it into his pocket. He started examining the materials in the folder as he walked across the top of the building to the helicopter.

Jonathan cleared his throat. "Can you imagine the piece of shit who thought setting a global killer loose was a good idea? God, I hope he rots in hell."

Gabriel shook his head, smiling. There didn't seem to be anything that Jonathan could say that would remotely begin to make him be liked. He nodded to Jonathan saying, "That's only if hell will take him."

Jonathan smiled nervously, staring at the helicopter pad and the chopper that sat on it, realizing that he was going to be in close quarters with this very scary man for the foreseeable future. Jonathan asked, "You got a plan figured out for what you want to do?"

Gabriel nodded at Jonathan. He was still staring at the folder and was looking over all of the details given to him by Frank. Jonathan sat there for a moment waiting for the engine to warm up and doing final system checks on the helicopter, hoping that, given enough time, Gabriel would come around and break that tough shell. Unfortunately for Jonathan, it wasn't a shell; it was a rock-hard exterior and he didn't know the first thing about Gabriel. After another ten minutes, they had been approved for a flight plan and were on their way into hell's mouth.

Gabriel looked through the materials he'd been given, reading the history of the group stemming back to the early nineties. Hassan had been the original leader and founder of the group. The leadership role was then passed down to the hands of his western-educated son, Imad. He read deeper into the file and actually started to worry for the country if he failed. He saw that the men were poorly educated, with the exception of Imad, and believed in Hassan's view Allah and in the group's mission. He looked over at his pilot, who looked like he had a brick squeezed tight in his ass. He said, "Hey take it easy. You're my pilot, right?"

Jonathan nodded his head. "Yeah, that seems to be the case, currently."

Gabriel said, "If it makes you feel any better, I've never shot one of my pilots mid-mission."

Jonathan nodded, looking a bit easier about things until the word "mid" hit him. "Wait, what do you mean 'mid'?"

Gabriel laid his head back and closed his eyes, trying to think for a moment about getting some type of plan together. "Do me a favor, kid. Shut up and let me think. We're going into a foreign-run factory, probably filled to the brink with all kinds of mass-produced, dangerous chemicals and shit, and we have to worry about every man and woman in there wanting to put a bullet through our skulls."

"Wait. What am I going to be doing while you are inside of this facility? I mean, I don't have shit for tactical experience. You don't want me going in there with you, do you? I will if you need me to, but I'd probably be a better shield than helper."

Gabriel looked at the skinny young man. "You wearing a vest, kid?"

The young man shook his head no and said, "Why's that?"

"Well, if you're going to be a shield you'd do a hell of a lot better if you had a bulletproof vest. I mean, if they shoot you in the chest, those bullets are just going to go straight through you, man. Hell, you probably couldn't even stop a small caliber handgun. If you had a vest and were in front of me, at least you'd stand a chance. Hell, I never leave home without one and I at least know what I'm doing in the field. How the fuck are you the best that they got at the CIA?"

Jonathan just gaped. "You know, absolutely none of that made me feel one damn bit better."

They flew in silence for the next few hours. Gabriel shrugged, looking through binoculars at the countryside in front of the building they were about to try to break into. He scanned the area, seeing it was desolate for miles around; they didn't want any chance at letting someone sneak up on them. He said, "You know, this set up is damn smart. If I wanted to make sure I didn't have any visitors, I'd put my place out in the middle of nowhere as well; that way, anyone who shows up uninvited, wouldn't belong there, and I would deem them hostile.

"So, what are you going to do?"

Gabriel kept staring into the distance, knowing it would be impossible to get in there without some sort of distraction. "Well, I was thinking that if a pilot tried landing in there without permission, they would go apeshit, and all their attention would be on that poor bastard."

Jonathan looked over, shaking his head. Gabriel said, "Did you want to call Frank and let him know that you aren't able to help complete the mission? You want the epidemic to be unleashed… to spread?"

"Well, no, but it seems like a damn death trap."

"I could always just kill you now, jump out of the chopper, and let you crash on the other side of the building and then run up while they are none the wiser."

Jonathan looked around the copter, realizing there was no way to stop Gabriel from doing whatever he decided to do. "So, you want me to drop you off somewhere before I go land the chopper? You'd better live up to your name, sir."

Gabriel gave him the most serious look that he could and said, "No one has ever regretted putting their trust in me, Jonathan. I always come through."

"And they all, you know, uh… they lived, right?"

Gabriel nodded, pointing to a strip of land to bring the helicopter down.

Chapter 9
Allah's Hand

Iran, Terror Cell Headquarters (twelve months prior)
October 14, 2023

The leaders, Imad Al-Din and his father, Hassan, the

founder of the group, sat around the table. Hassan held up his hands in frustration, looking up to the ceiling and praying for Allah to give him the answers that he needed. To his son, he screamed, "Why do your plans have to be so damn complicated? What is wrong with my plan? Why must you disrespect me at all times, Imad?

"It is not that I am trying to disrespect you, sir. I would never do that to you, Father. I respect you very, very much."

Hassan snapped back with what he always relied on and yelled, "You spent too long at the University in England. You act like one of them now." He pointed to what Imad was wearing, a light-tan suit, and then motioned at himself wearing his army fatigues. "You dress like one of those of those pieces of shit. If it was not for my blood moving through your veins, I would happily slit your throat as a sacrifice to Allah."

"Father, it is what I have learned speaking with the scientists who believe in our cause. They call it biological warfare. They say we can change a virus. We can modify it and make it something that cannot be cured or stopped. It will be the greatest accomplishment of Allah's Hand to date, Father."

"That is stupid. Americans cure everything but the fucking debt. They can always save others as long as you are one of their precious citizens."

"Father, not this one. They told me that we need a scientist whose profession is researching drugs and diseases. We need a strand as well, like a sample of the strain's disease. We need a place for him to work at and then—"

Hassan was losing his mind with what he felt was disrespectful behavior from his only son. He slammed both hands on the table. "We do all this work for a few thousand people to die maybe? Why does this leave hundreds of millions still alive to infect the world?"

Imad smiled, showing off very white teeth in contrast to his dark-amber skin. "No, Father, I mean no disrespect when I say this, but you do not understand what I mean or what I'm talking about. The applications of this would not just lead to a few thousand deaths, you see; it would bring America to her knees. They would not be able to bury the bodies fast enough. They would run out of room before they were done... or even out of people to bury them."

"You never make any sense. You know this, right? I blame your whore of a mother. You would still be on her tit if I had not taken care of her."

"Father, what I speak is the truth. I do not mean like a Nine-Eleven or the Oklahoma bombing."

"Why don't you save us both time and say what you mean."

Imad shook his head, past the point of trying to explain what he felt was stupidly simple to comprehend. "Sorry, Father, but I can't be led by a fool any longer."

"Good! I am glad that we are done talking about this foolish..." It hit him what he had just been told, the disrespect slapping him in the face. He pulled a knife from his belt and waved it in the air. "You call me a fool? You son of a whore. I will cut your tongue out! I will slit you from top to bottom! Your new way of thinking is more than my old ears can handle!"

"Can I tell you one thing I've learned, Father, please?"

His father flung his chair, kicking it as he started his approach across the room to his son. He screamed, "You let your last words be what you choose them to be. What difference does it make to me?"

Imad sat back calmly in his chair. He raised a silenced pistol and aimed it directly at his father's chest. He said, "In America, they say do not a bring a knife to a gunfight."

Hassan stopped in his approach. He tilted his head to the side. "I don't understand what that means."

Imad shook his head in astonishment. How could one man be so powerful and so ignorant at the exact same time? "Have Allah explain it to you."

He pulled the trigger twice and rose to his feet. His father's eyes bugged out and he stumbled backwards, dropping his knife. He tried to reach for his pistol, but Imad was on his feet and stripped him of it. He helped his father back up into a wheeled chair as smoke rose from his chest. Hassan was shaking in the chair, filled with fear of death and rage for his son's unbelievable betrayal. Imad opened the office door and looked to see if any of the men had been lingering in the hallway outside awaiting further orders. He knew that Allah was shining down on him today because he saw no one.

When he turned around to wheel his father into the hallway, he saw that blood was coming from the sides of his cheeks when he attempted to speak. It poured out, soaking his front and he said, "Why Imad? Why would you betray me like this? You are not strong enough to do this on your own. You will fail. You cannot be a leader; you are too young and too weak. You will fail, you coward!"

Imad smiled and patted his father's shoulder as his eyes began to glaze. "Father, if I am the weak one then why are you the one who is sitting in the chair with bullet wounds?"

As Hassan opened his mouth one final time to speak, the blood gurgled as he slipped into the great unknown. Imad pushed him across the hallway and to the elevator. He wheeled his father inside and punched the button to go to the bottom floor. He waited, watching the floors, nervously knowing the allegiance that most of the men had was to his father and not wanting to run into any of them. He knew that it was going to take a miracle to pull this off. The elevator doors dinged and opened. Imad stuck his head out and looked both ways down the hall.

Again, he felt that Allah was shining on him when he saw only Fahid who was, by far, one of his most trusted and faithful men. He screamed for the man down the long hall. "Fahid are you alone? Is there anyone else in the hall with you?"

Fahid gave a thumbs up and smiled proudly while waving and shaking his head. "Hello Imad, what are you doing? Do you need help, my friend?"

Imad motioned with his hand to urgently come to him. "Fahid, come here now. I do need help. I need your help very much and now please."

The man listened and obeyed. He ran towards the elevator and about fell in shock when he saw the leader. "Oh my god, Imad! What the hell happened to your father? Did you do this, Imad?"

"He didn't understand evolution. He didn't understand the big picture... that we are capable of so much more... the things that we could do."

"I can keep your secret, Imad. I will be your left hand man. What is it that you think that we can do?" He pounded his chest in comradely.

Imad did not correct him; he knew that it was pointless. The two of them wheeled his dad's corpse out the back door where his father kept a car that was always gassed up and ready to flee if need be.

Imad looked out the back door that led to the alleyway. When he was confident that the coast was clear, he motioned for Fahid to come out the door. The two men kept his father steady as they quickly wheeled the chair outside. Imad yelled, "We must get him out of here before anyone sees him! Fahid, I need you to drive him and his car to a garage or parking lot—somewhere that he will be left alone. He needs to be out of sight for a while."

Fahid opened the passenger door and the two men hoisted Hassan up, sliding him into the passenger seat. Imad held his father in place while Fahid secured the seat belt to keep him upright. Imad pulled out a set of keys and tossed them to Fahid. "Fahid, I need to go back inside. You come back as soon as you secure him somewhere. Hurry please; we don't have much time. We don't want people wondering where you've gone to."

Fahid smiled proudly, accepting the keys. "I am going to protect you from evil, Imad. I will not let harm find you. You are our savior; you will protect us and rid us of all the infidels that plague the world."

Imad nodded. "You will be great. Now go now and stop for nothing, speak to no one."

Fahid ran around the side of the car and climbed into the driver's seat. He turned the car over and Fahid sped down the alleyway. As the car began to turn the corner, Imad pulled a black box from his pocket and pushed a red button. His father's car exploded, sending it ten feet into the air. Black smoke rolled up in waves. The force from the explosion charred both men to a point where they wouldn't be recognizable. The buildings running parallel had scorch marks going up them as well.

When Imad was content that it had definitely taken care of them, he turned and sprinted to the building, taking the stairs as quickly as his smoker's lungs would allow. When he knew he was out of sight, he hit his radio, screaming, "Someone tell me what that was! Are we being attacked? What is happening outside?"

The radio chatter came back with too many voices trying to talk over each other. Imad screamed, "Shut up, all of you! Everyone stop talking! I can't understand you all screaming at once! Now one of you answer! What is going on outside?"

Ali, one of his father's guards came back over the radio, sounding very nervous to be delivering the bad news. "This is Ali here. I am outside in the alleyway and, Imad, I am sorry to say it looks as if those pieces of shits got him."

Imad played his part the best that he could. "They got who, Ali? Who? You are making no fucking sense."

"Imad, it is your father's car and there are two men inside. It is impossible to know who they are, but one of them is wearing your father's necklace."

Imad screamed at the top of his lungs. "They will pay! We will take care of them all! Clean the computers now! Bring the hard drives and burn this building to the ground! We will continue in my father's footsteps."

Ali asked over the walkie-talkie, "What is our next goal? What do we do from here?"

Imad yelled, "We stop talking on walkie-talkies, you fucking moron. Are you trying to get a bomb dropped on our heads?"

The men were quiet. They knew that the words he was saying were true. It would not be the first time the military had done such an act. Ali quickly and quietly said, "Everyone do your job and meet at the backup site."

Imad said, "We will meet as soon as you complete your jobs. I have wonderful news to share with all of you."

The radio stayed quiet this time and Imad made his way back to the office where he had spilled his father's blood. He did his part of the emergency evacuation drill and sprayed the room with a can of gasoline that was kept for such a specific chain of events. He tossed a match on the table, lighting the papers and gasoline ablaze. He watched the men running through the halls, taking care of their specific duties. He felt confident that, even if it had been the Americans who blew up the car and were trying to take them down, they would still be safe

Imad ran down the steps and to a car that he kept for himself if he needed to leave in a hurry—a lesson he had learned and found valuable. He was the first one to the backup site and had the generators fired up and electricity started by the time that the rest of the men arrived. They had, unfortunately, done it enough times that they were now pros at getting the computer equipment set up. Within a few hours, they had the backup site ready to go and back online. He called the men in, organizing them into a small room. When they were gathered and seated, Ali raised his hand before Imad was able to begin his speech. Imad pointed to the man, nodding. "What? How can you have questions? I've only just brought you in here for, god sakes."

"Imad, from the bottom of my heart I… I mean from all of ours, we wish to tell you how sorry we are that this happened."

Imad nodded his head, walking around the room. He patted Ali on the shoulder. "Thank you, Ali, but this would have never happened had we started my father's plan a year ago."

"What plan is that, Imad? He had not mentioned anything that was new to any of us, at least that I know of."

"He had a stroke of genius in his final talk with me this afternoon." Imad pulled out a brown folder and passed out the contents to the men. Each man scrolled through the sheets, seeing different pictures of a man; in some of the pictures, he was alone and in others, with his family.

The men were clueless and looked at him, confused. Ali cleared his throat and asked, "Imad, who the fuck is this man? He looks like a scientist. Is he going to begin building our new bombs? How is blowing shit up going to be anything different than the plans which your father usually presents to us?"

The rest of the men laughed lightly, knowing it was true. Imad smiled too; he knew fear would be one of the things that would make his men respect him. He was confident that another would be because of his new ideas. Imad lifted his pistol and aimed it dead center at Ali's head. Ali saw this and stopped smiling immediately as his jaw dropped and began to quiver. He held both hands out in front of him. "Imad, don't; I beg of you, please. I was only joking! I did not mean any disrespect from it. I swear to you. I swear!"

Imad fired the pistol once, sending the bullet through one of the man's palms and into and out the back of his skull. Blood and brains sprayed the wall behind him as the shell casing spun on the cheap table's top. While the gore slowly slid down the wall, Ali's hands dropped to his sides and his lifeless, limp body slumped to the left, slipping out of his chair and onto the ground.

The other men in the group, who apparently didn't believe he was going to fire the pistol, had jumped a foot back from Ali. Imad did not lower the gun; he pointed it at the other men. "My father was a great man, and we will honor him as such. Does anyone have anything else to say about him, or are you ready to get to work?"

The men sat back down, trying their best—but failing miserably—to ignore the man who was bleeding on the floor near their feet. "This is Dr. Abul; he is one of the leading men in his field. He is going to make Allah's Hand remembered until the end of time."

A man raised a shaking hand. He was terrified that Imad was going to give him a repeat performance of what his fallen brother had just received minutes before. Imad did not want to lose his momentum, but could not ignore the man and the horrid face that he was making. "What do you want, Mohammed? You look like you are going to shit yourself. Did you shit yourself already?"

Mohammed sat up straight in his seat, shaking his head. "I just wanted to know what we need to kidnap a doctor for?"

"He is going to take us to new levels. He is a master of what he does. We aren't going to be able to do this without him."

Mohammed interrupted, "I'm sorry, Imad, but I do not understand."

"Well, if you would just shut up, you might learn something."

"Oh my… a thousand apologies, sir."

"Keep them. Just shut up! I do not want any more interruptions. If given the proper resources and time, he will supply us with a strand of disease so deadly that it will cripple America. They will not be able to stop us. Anyone who lives will be taken out after we release our super virus."

"The others in the picture, what would you like us to do with them, sir? Do you want to take unnecessary hostages?"

Imad answered, "I want you to enter the home and restrain the good doctor and his family. I will enter not very far behind you."

*****

Dr. Akbar Abul's Family Residence, two days later

Dr. Abul was only half-paying attention to his driving. He had disease on the mind, as usual, and spoke into a voice recorder, knowing that if he waited, he would to forget his ideas. The future scared him gravely. If only people were aware of what could become of society if even the weakest strand of a deadly disease is introduced into the population.

He shook his thoughts free when he saw his driveway and hit his remote to open the large, metal double gate. He looked around, making sure there were no little ones in the driveway riding their tricycles, and pulled his Mercedes into the wide driveway, steering clear of an overturned tricycle. He grabbed his briefcase, knowing he would be working late into the evening. He hit his car alarm, in case one of the local looters made it over the fence somehow, and headed inside.

His children rushed towards him, smiling, and screaming, thrilled that their father was home. He opened his arms wide as the kids came rushing around the corner, and wrapped his arms around them in a massive group hug. The three kids pushed him over and the four of them rolled on the ground laughing.

His wife, Abrisham, leaned against the doorway, shaking her head. "Do I have three children or do I have four? You children go back and finish your studies for the night and let your father in the door."

She walked over and picked up his briefcase and suit coat, then put them in their proper places. Akbar pushed up from the ground, feeling the little pains in his knees and back that did not exist before the two had wedded and had children. Abrisham gave him a hug and kissed his cheek. "How was your day today, Akbar?"

Akbar knew that she was just being nice and really didn't want a full explanation of the horribly complicated science he'd been working with all day. So, he simply replied, "It was good. No one died working with disease strands and we all went home."

She shook her head, trying to hold back a smile at his daily joke. "You know you could have just simply been a doctor who performed medical needs for people, and then I would not have to worry about you and your health and the health of our children."

Akbar shrugged. "Well, I am much too old now to do anything about it, Abrisham. You know what they say about old dogs in America, don't you?"

Abrisham, who was very well adapted to some of the ways of the west smiled, reaching and tugging at her husband's belt and sliding her hands down his pants. "Oh, I do not believe you are that old, are you?"

Akbar smiled, looking into his wife's dark-brown eyes and seeing the passion in them that he was very accustomed to seeing. He rubbed her arm up and down smoothly, tickling more than touching. "What are we going to do with the children? You know the minute we start, they are going to rush in, do you not?"

She smiled and pulled him towards the winding staircase by his pants and looked over at him with nothing less than seduction. "I rented them an American cartoon movie. They are going to be watching it for the next two hours."

Akbar liked this idea and said, "Okay, well, will you go upstairs and get our shower going? I want to lock the front door and make sure the security system is on and active."

She was in a teasing mood and tilted her head playfully. "You aren't just thinking that maybe you'd like to come upstairs with me instead and take our chances? I don't think anyone will try and take our little heathens. I've been with them all day long and *I* wouldn't take them at this point."

Akbar smiled. "You love them and you know it, even if they do drive you crazy. You are a wonderful mother and a beautiful wife. Now, go get the shower nice and steamy. I have a few spots on my back that I am going to need help getting clean."

She patted the front of his pants, never faltering her smile. "Well, it seems like there might be a few places you might need help washing."

He thought about the alarm and thought they would probably be okay, but knew there were too many insane people in the country with radical ideas, so he should do the responsible thing. He leaned up and gave her a long, deep kiss, patted her on the backside, and said, "Don't get too hot without me. I will be back in two shakes."

Akbar smiled to himself, thinking of how great the rest of his night was going to be. He went by the living room and watched his children for a moment, smiling, and not for one moment forgetting how very lucky he was to have everyone in his life. He went to the front door and locked the deadbolt. What he saw next was so out of place that it seemed as if he was watching a dream.

A rusted-out military transport truck pulled up out of nowhere and in front of the double gates. Akbar watched in confusion as two men, both wearing masks and military uniforms, came from behind the truck where they worked like pros. The first man hit a latch to release a cable attached to the front of the truck. The second soon-to-be-intruder pulled the heavy-duty cable and wire in the direction that he was trying for. He wrapped it around where the two gates came together and set the hook. The two men ran out of the way, slamming on the hood to let the driver know that they would be clear. The two men both caught assault rifles that were thrown from someone who was in the back. The large diesel truck shifted into reverse, accelerating quickly and pulled the gate from its hinges.

After a moment, it broke from its place and the truck pulled it free and back twenty feet. Akbar screamed to his wife, who by now, he figured, was naked and in the shower. He ran outside, waving his hands in the air and shaking his fists. "What do you think you are doing? Get off of my property right now you pieces of shits. There are people living here! Take your crazy asses somewhere else now or I will call the police, I swear it to Allah."

The children ran outside and the look that Akbar gave them was more than enough to make them reconsider their actions. The three turned on their heels and sprinted back inside the house. The oldest screamed to the younger siblings, "Get back inside, now, now!" Then to his father, "We are sorry, we just wanted to see what the commotion outside was about. Why did they tear our fence down, Father? Are they going to hurt us?"

Akbar, who did not want to scare his children, lied. "Don't be silly, son. Why would they want to hurt us? We have done nothing to harm them, have we?

The boy shrugged, looking at the men and seeing that there were no signs of kindness in their eyes or expressions on their faces. The fact that they wore masks made the child even more nervous about them. The boy yelled one last question as the men approached, "If they do not come to harm us, Father, then why are they here? What do they want?"

His father raised a firm hand and snapped, "Get inside now, or feel pain, boy! Go now. I do not know the answers to these questions, but I will soon. Get moving and do it now. Go… Go! Take your brother and sister upstairs and hide. I will come and find you later. I need you to move, and I need you to do it now."

The boy wasted no more time turning and running. Akbar watched as the young man obeyed, gripping the two little ones by their small hands, and dragged them upstairs to the bedrooms. Akbar screamed, "Do you hear me? Do you hear me? I will call the police! I will call right now if you do not leave. I am a very important man and you will be sorry if you do not go. Go now!"

The two men stood at the now open gates, aiming their rifles at Akbar. They looked behind them as the truck came to a stop and everyone, but the driver, came out of the truck. They disconnected the cables from the gate while another hit the winch to retrieve it. Six of them sprinted to the front of the door. Akbar saw the masked men coming at him, carrying assault rifles, and wasted no more time waiting. He turned and slammed the door, securing all of the locks. He hit the emergency alarm switch and prayed that there would be enough time before these men infiltrated the house.

He sprinted up the stairs as quickly as he could but did not make it halfway up the flight before machine gun fire erupted. He crouched on the stairs. The door handles all but vanished as blasts fired, one after another. He looked over his shoulder and saw the door fly open and a black military boot coming through. Akbar stopped trying to flee the men. He came down the steps slowly but cautiously. Four of the men ran up the steps and pulled him down by his shirt, his feet dragging down the steps. Akbar was screaming, "What? What do you want, god damn you?"

Akbar tried to push up to his feet and one of the men pushed him back down with a heavy foot. Akbar saw the men heading up the steps and he screamed, "No!" as he tried to push back up. This time the man took the butt of his rifle and brought it down hard against the side of his head. Akbar dropped to the ground; his head was swimming as he fought to stay conscious. He tried lifting his head, but the man put a foot on top of his chest, which took little pressure to keep the doctor down at this point.

This all changed when they dragged a soaking-wet Abrisham, who had nothing more than a towel that she was clinging to for dear life. Two men clung to her arms leaving marks as they dragged her down the steps, leaving a water trail. "Akbar, Akbar… What did you do to him? Why is he bleeding, you monsters?"

The men dragging her felt that women were little more than a vessel to produce offspring, and they ignored her screams and pleas. When she wouldn't end her screams, one of the men brought up a large hand and punched her in the face, splitting her cheek open. They threw her in the corner, keeping a gun trained on her, and telling her to not move.

Akbar shook his head, knowing that the blood was not flowing through his brain like it should be. He was confident that a concussion, if he lived through the day, was going to be inevitable. He could only watch as one of the intruders threw his wife into the corner.

Imad walked in looking around; he saw the wife in the towel and the bleeding doctor on the ground. Imad screamed, "What are you doing? Did I tell any of you to hurt him? He is a doctor! If you damage his brain, what good is to me? I do not need any more brainless men working for me."

The doctor pushed up and sat where he fell. "I do not and will not work for you. I do not know who you are and I do not care. You need to leave and you need to do so now. I have set off the police alarm and they will be here soon. I think that you are making a grave mistake. One that I think you will regret for many moons to come, sir."

Imad shrugged and knelt down next to Akbar. Imad handed him a folded silk handkerchief for his head, which the doctor took with a shaky hand. "We know exactly who you are, Dr. Akbar Abul. You are head of the Hematology Department for the Department of Health and Standards. You are a quite talented doctor, especially when it comes to diseases and how to cure them."

"What do you want? You waste my time. You frighten my family and disrespect my wife. You need to leave now. I will do nothing that you ask of me."

"You do not want to think over what I propose? You are so quick to deny, without knowing what it is that I require."

"There is nothing you will want that will not be filled with sin. You scream bad intentions."

Imad pulled his pistol and aimed it at his wife. "You are sure that you will not change your mind, doctor? There are no second chances when it comes to life and death. Can you handle living without her?"

Akbar screamed, "You don't have the—"

Imad never let him finish his sentence. He aimed at the wife who was on her knees, clutching the towel to her chest, screaming "No!" Imad pulled the trigger once, sending an echoing bullet noise through the home. The large-caliber pistol round slammed her back against the wall. She went instantly limp as her head exploded from the back. Akbar screamed in rage, sounding more animal than human. Imad never raised his pulse; he knelt back down by the doctor and patted him on the shoulder. "I am very sorry that we had to do this. But, doctor, I need your help, and you are not being very helpful. You will not even be rational about listening to me."

"What… what else can you take from me? She was my life… my love… she was everything to me."

Imad patted him on the shoulder. He looked to one of his men and pointed upstairs. "Go up and retrieve the children. They were here when you arrived, weren't they?"

The man nodded and Imad pointed to go get them and to do it quickly. Akbar could not take his tear-filled eyes off of his wife. Abrisham lay there hunched over in a heap, the white Egyptian towel now soaked through with her blood. Imad asked, "Would this go any easier if we were to just start killing your children one by one? You have three of them, do you not?"

Akbar could not stop the tears from falling. "Yes, I have two sons and a daughter. But you already know all of this, don't you? You have something horrible in mind that you are wishing to have happen, aren't you? You have an evil purpose in mind for which I am specialized."

Imad smiled, looking up at his men. "You see. I told you that the doctor was smart. He knows what we might do, what we could think of to do to his children if he disobeys. Oh, the things that creative visionaries like us could be capable of coming up with."

"If you hurt any of them, I will slit my own throat and you will not get what you want. At least you will not get it from me. You can look elsewhere, but I assure you that I am the best in my field, and I will be able to do what others only dream of."

"You can say that without me even telling you what I need? That is a very impressive statement you are making. We will be filling you in on the plane ride. We need you to be somewhere you will be able to concentrate and have the amenities which you'll require to perform tests and research."

"I have a lab that, I am sure you are aware, is state of the art. There is nothing I can't accomplish there. You can take me there and I can do what it is that you think you need."

"We are going to America. We will be leaving in a few hours' time. My men will go upstairs and get some things for you and the children. You will need them in the coming months."

"'Coming months' and 'America'? What the hell do you think I am going to do?"

Imad smiled, helping the man to his feet, then put on a pair of handcuffs to keep the doctor from acting out. "That is very simple, doctor. You are going to work with a disease of my choosing and you are going to modify it to a point where they will not be able to cure anyone who is infected with it."

"You are interested in this being in America because why?"

"Because they do not deserve to live! We are going to cure the world of their filth and disease. We will cure the world. We will receive much praise from Allah, and we will see the heavens when we are gone from this world."

"You are insane! You aren't thinking clearly! You cannot kill a country."

Imad walked to the stairs, grabbed one of the children by the arm, and yanked him down the rest of the way. The small boy began screaming for his father to help him. Imad slapped him and threw him to the ground. When Akbar reached for his son, Imad kicked him in the face, sending blood from a freshly broken nose all across the tiled marble floors. Akbar said, "I will do what you want. I will do what you want... just leave my son alone... please, I beg you... I beg you!"

Imad held his pistol to the young boy's temple. "Are you sure that you are going to be able to do what we want? That there will be no more issues from you?"

Akbar held up his hand. "I swear to you, I will do nothing else. I will be at your command until the mission is complete. I beg you. I promise you! Please do not do that—I would not be able to go on!"

Imad pulled the pistol back from the boy's head. He threw him into his father's chest. Akbar stared with a hatred he'd never known he was capable of feeling while holding his son in a deep hug. Imad screamed to the rest of the men. "Round up what we need! Bring the doctor's computer and his files and books. I want him to have everything that he needs to have. You need to get moving. The police will be here soon and if we can leave before they arrive that would be best."

The crew walked out, escorting what was left of the Abul family. When they made it outside, they saw that the gunshots inside the home had been enough to make the neighbors come outside in curiosity. They stood in the street, speaking to one another and gossiping about what was happening in the doctor's home. When they saw six heavily armed guards escorting out the family, they turned and ran into their houses, slamming the doors and wasting no time calling the police themselves. Imad ushered the family up into the back of the truck, and as he and his men were climbing into it, the police rounded the corner. Three squad cars sped down the doctor's street and parked at an angle, slamming on their brakes, skidding the vehicles, and blocking the giant diesel military transport truck from going anywhere.

The squad cars opened their doors and the police officers rushed out of them. They did not know who they were dealing with; when they started yelling orders for them to let the hostages go, and lie down in the street with their hands behind their backs, all hell broke loose. Imad and his men brought up their hands, but only for a millisecond while each of the four men threw a grenade. The small metal grenades flew into the air, bounced along the street, and rolled to a stop beneath the cars. Within seconds, the grenades went off and exploded, followed immediately by more blasts from the cars' gas tanks. The officers who were still inside the three cars never had a chance. Those who were out of the cars before the grenades exploded were left dazed, confused, and bleeding.

Imad brought up a large belt-fed machine gun, aimed it at the police and unleashed hell's fire on them, cutting the men still alive in half with fifty-caliber bullets. By the time the belt was empty, there was nothing left of the men on the ground. At least that would be able to be put back together again. Blood and guts littered the streets. The driver brought the giant diesel to life and they reversed the truck, angling it down the street, and brought it to full speed. The ancient military truck dominated what was left of the small police cars, smashing directly into them and spinning them sideways upon impact.

The vehicle sped down the street, not stopping until they reached the hangar of the airplane that was ready to start their long and careful trip into the United States. When they made it stateside, the doctor and his family were locked in a laboratory where all research of the deadly virus would take place. After settling into the facility, Dr. Abul was presented with five different diseases that he could pick from and was made aware that, if he failed, what was left of his family would have indescribable and unimaginable things happen to them, slowly and surely.

The doctor worked on his own for the next twelve months. The terrorists advised him daily what they would do to his family if they did not see results. The doctor worked to the brink of going insane. He knew in his heart that every day he worked brought them one step closer to the destruction of the government and the crippling of an entire continent... or possibly worse.

*****

Imad was going over research reports from the doctor. His ideas were great, his research brilliant, and what he was doing had never been done before. He sat back in his seat thinking about the day that he would bring them to their knees, all because of his ideas. Imad knew he would be curing the world. That when the infidels were cast into hell, and he and his brothers were sent to heaven to live in peace with Allah, it would all be worth it.

Mohammed knocked on the door. He had been bitter ever since coming here; all of the men had. They had complained about having to shave their beards and hair. They had been made to give up their military fatigues and weapons that they carried around on a daily basis. They had been working in various jobs around the company doing remedial janitorial work while awaiting news from the doctor that he had finally finished what they had asked of him.

The knock startled Imad out of his trance-like state. He turned around in his seat, rising to his feet and looking down the hall over Mohammed's shoulder. "Did anyone see you come up to the office? You know that you are not supposed to come here while the staff is working. We are here as a favor to Allah's Hand. We do not want to make anyone here pissed off. It would not be easy to move the doctor and his family, along with all of the research projects in their current states."

"This is important. I did not think that you would want to wait to hear this."

"What is so important that you needed to interrupt me? I was looking at Dr. Abul's research and I was—"

"Damn it sir, please listen to me, Imad! He has done it. He thinks that he is there. He said that he has a room full of dead animals. He thinks that he is ready to attempt human testing."

Imad smiled and his eyes glowed. He walked back and forth, shaking his hands in victory in the air and putting his hands together and praising Allah. "Mohammed, you have made me very happy. I want you to gather the employees and bring them down to the lab."

Mohammed turned to leave and stopped, turning back around to ask him, "Imad, I know a person is a person, but was there some sort of type that you are looking at getting? Does it matter what we get for test subjects?"

Imad stared around the office, thinking of the five hundred and twenty-eight million citizens. He said slyly, "I want you to get all the men with brown hair and brown eyes. I want their women that have blonde hair and blue eyes. We will get Jesus and see if their God can make them live; if their God can save them."

Mohammed laughed, smiling ear to ear. "I like that. I like that a lot. We will put their God out there; we will see if they live. What will happen when hell strikes fury down upon them? When it is their time to be judged; will they die or will they prosper?"

Imad slapped him on the shoulder. "They will die and they will be judged. There will be no salvation for the weak; they will perish. I want you to put them in a conference room,

out of the way, until everyone else leaves."
*****

Later that night, when those who had not been called into a special meeting had left the building, the factory had turned into a place of hell. Imad and his men unlocked the conference door. The group had taken the room earlier in the day stripping it of all phones and setting up a cell phone blocker for anyone who had tried to sneak one in. They stared in disbelief when the men who had taken them hostage earlier in the day came back in with their military fatigues on and assault rifles in hand. One of the employees understood that something was horribly wrong but still missed the severity of it. He smiled nervously at Imad and held up his hand. When no one paid attention to him, he cleared his throat. "Uh, hello, sir, do you speak English?"

Imad stared at the intrusion on him and his men. He walked over to the man who did not understand what was going on and before he could speak, the man looked to another of the hostages and whispered, "I do not think that they speak English. Leave it to terrorists to take hostages and not know the language."

The woman he was speaking to said, "Why are you whispering if they don't speak English?"

Imad leaned in a little closer, holding his rifle tightly, and in a British accent said, "Because he is a moron and just wants to assume that men from Iran, holding rifles, who have taken him and his fellow employees hostage must be too ignorant to speak English."

The man's mouth dropped. "Uh, yeah, so sorry about that. It was nothing personal, Mr.—?"

Imad took the rifle's butt stock and smashed it into the man's ribs. He gasped for air, dropping to the ground and holding his ribs tightly. Imad said, "Did you have any more questions?"

"I... I just want to know what you want. What are your demands and why are you here?"

"We have no demands, you piece of shit."

"So, if you don't want anything, then what are we are supposed to do for you? How do we resolve this?"

"There is no resolve. You can do only one thing for me useful. Now get on your feet and move. We have very much work to do. We have a busy week ahead of us." Imad pointed at two of his men. "You two make sure we are not interrupted. We will be closed for business tomorrow. Put a sign on the front door; send out an email advising people the plant has shut down because of an accident. If anyone comes to the doors to try and go to work in the morning, put a bullet through them."

Both men pounded their chests and turned and ran out of sight. Imad and the other four men forced the hostages out of the room and down the hall. The non-elected speaker for the group asked, "Where are we going? If you don't want anything from us what reason do you have to keep us, damn it? This is America and we have rights here. We have rights, damn you!"

Imad thought about the tests and realized they did not need quite this many people. He gripped the man by the back of his collar, turned him, and pushed him back into the conference room. He said, "The reason that we had taken them is because we mean to kill you. We have been using your facility for quite some time with the help of its owners and scientists. You Americans did not see us because we were just lowly janitors, cooks, and mechanics; men like you felt that we did not warrant your respect."

The man was looking increasingly nervous being alone with him. "Then what were you doing all these months?"

Imad smiled and brought out a large tactical knife, showing it to the man who flinched at the sight of it so near his face. He tried to put his hands up in front of his face, but they were zip tied behind his back and made it an impossible feat to be done. "That is a very easy question with a very complicated answer. We brought an Iranian scientist here; he is a genius of a man. We have modified a disease to kill all of your people. You will all die and there will be no survivors."

"What do you mean all of my people? Are you talking about a biological attack on America?"

"Yes. And you… well, not you so much, but your colleagues, have all got a special part to play today. Depending on the outcome, there is a good chance that we will be able to move forth with it very, very soon."

The man said, "You are going to use us as test subjects?"

Imad brought the knife up quickly, slicing through the front of the man's neck. Blood poured from it, changing the color of his shirt forever and the man's fate. Imad smiled and wiped the blade on the man's suit coat. "You did not listen; you will not be a subject. No, you will just die. Consider this a gift. The pain that your friends will incur is going to be much more painful to deal with."

The man opened his mouth to attempt to speak, but only blood came out, gurgling his words. Imad pushed the man over, smiling, looking at his blade, and thinking of how very primitive the kill had been. "If only it could have been this easy, then my father would be here today to bask in our glory with us."

He stared into the man's eyes and watched the light in them fade away into nothing.

*****

Imad walked quickly to catch up to the group. He knew he was close when he heard the pleas and whimpering of the walking dead. There would be no place in the world to hide, once he unleashed this on society. There would be consequences to hell and back for the actions that he would set in motion today. He believed in Allah and knew that he was on the mission of the righteous and Allah would take care of them. Allah would see to it that they would survive today and many more days to come. Imad knew that if he could unleash this on America, then the rest of the world would be much easier to conquer. The interconnected Europe would crumble. The dead would lie in the streets, spreading their diseases to others.

As Imad caught up to them, the hostages were refusing to go into the sterile room. Imad screamed at them, waving his pistol in the air. They figured they would die by these men's hands one way or another. Imad walked up and pistol-whipped two of the men across the back of their heads, making their legs go limp and falling to the ground. Imad screamed at his men, "Are you trying to let them get away and escape, damn it? Get these fools into the room now! We are too close to fail! Unless, of course, you would like to take their places?"

The men looked at each other nervously and gripped the fallen men by their necks and threw them into the room. The hostages screamed and punched on the double-sided mirror in the observation room. Imad's men held their guns on them while the others secured the doors.

Dr. Abul watched as the men and women were marched into the room. It was a clean room with zero germs. They had made sure it was perfect. There was a ventilation filter to keep the germs, and any air breathed in and out, from going into the rest of the facility or the outside. Even though the facility was far enough out in the middle of nowhere, they still were not ready to make the country crumble.

They went to the observation room that housed Dr. Abul. He was sitting, looking over his final check of the research. Imad walked over and grabbed them from him before he could finish his notes. "Do you have it working now?" Imad asked.

The doctor looked up, more tired and with more loss than he had ever felt in his life. He longed for his days in Iran with his family and wife. He remembered back when they were all happy and alive, living simple day-to-day existences. On nights when his captors allowed him to sleep, his dreams were nightmares, plagued with the sight of his wife being shot in the head in front of his own eyes.

Imad stared intently at the research papers before saying anything else. "This research is good; this is very good. I think you have finally made a breakthrough, doctor. We have some more specimens to try your virus on."

Akbar looked up curiously. The window curtains were pulled closed and the glass was so thick that a truck could smash into. He said, "Yes I need to get more rabbits or rats please. I have gotten rid of almost all of them, and very soon I will be out."

"The men said that you are almost done. That is, if you are not done with the disease already."

The doctor stood, pushing up and away from the desk. He stretched his back and cracked his neck and fingers. "Yes, I believe we are near completion. I do not think that we need very much longer before you are ready, sir."

"Doctor, are you trying to postpone the inevitable? How much longer do you think we'll wait for you to accomplish what you are working towards?"

"Imad, I do not know how many more threats I can handle. I have lived in fear every day of my life since the day that you came into it. I do not need this; my children are living in darkness, not knowing their father—why they never see me or their mother. Why they aren't in a home. So, please don't take this for disrespect when I say that I think an existence in death, at this point, would be much less than what I am going through today."

Imad shook his head, smiling. "It is too bad that you aren't having fun anymore. I wish that you were still enjoying yourself. You are going to be the most famous of scientists that have ever lived. Everyone will know who you are and exactly what it was that you did. They are going to cheer your name in our homeland and fear your existence in all others. They will not know what to do to survive or what they can do to hide. They will perish while we rise to greatness."

"My children, Imad. That is all that I care about. I do

not want any credit for the evil that I've put together. There will be almost no one left once this has taken place. I want to see my children. I want to know how we are going to get out of the United States once this takes place."

Imad walked to the window and turned around. He smiled and said, "Your children are safe; we have kept them that way because we believe in you. I did not ever say anything about a ride back from the United States. I only promised you a ride here; I never said anything about you getting back home. You doctors, you are all so greedy."

As the doctor rose to his feet, Imad pointed his gun at him. "After all of this, do you want to leave your children orphans and alone? Is that what you want? You have done enough that I think either way we will be able to figure out what we need to do so that we can send the disease out."

He sat back down and raised his hands in defeat. "I am sorry. I will do what you ask; I cannot put my children through this. I must do what I can and I will do everything to try and get them back to Iran where they will have a chance to be safe. Are you planning on anywhere but America? I wish that you would reconsider this, but I know that you will not."

"After a year of pleading, I would think that you would give up." He pointed a finger up and down. "But you are one persistent son of a bitch, I give you credit for that. Your passion is what drives you. I am confident it is also what will kill you one day. Now, I want you to give me a sample of the drug for the clean room."

The doctor went to a large container, dipping in a small glass tube that held no more than two ounces of the potent liquid. He lifted it back out steadily and carefully, giving it the utmost respect that it deserved. He screwed on a top and pushed it into the wall to the observatory. He nodded to Imad, pointing to the button on the wall that would turn it into a gas form. "It is ready, Imad. Do you already have the animals in the room?"

Imad smiled and nodded while he hit the button that

would turn the liquid into a gas state. After it had a moment to begin filling the room, he opened the curtain. As the doctor peered into the dark room, Imad hit the lights, revealing the large group of people inside the room. They did not know what the cool mist was that was falling on their skin, but they were confident that nothing good would come out of tonight. The doctor screamed when he saw the people, tears instantly filling his eyes as he yelled, "What the hell is wrong with you? I thought you brought me specimens!"

Imad said, "Oh, but I did; the best kind."

"You have what you need, then. You have enough of it to end the world. Can I leave with my children, Imad… please? I have done everything that you…"

Imad laughed. "Of course, you cannot leave. We must sit together and watch the outcome. You would be heartbroken if you did not get to see the fruits of your labor in their final stages, would you not?"

Dr. Abul shook his head slowly, "No… no Imad, I believe that I can make do without seeing their pain."

Imad pointed at a metal seat. "Sit. I have grown tired of speaking to you. Always the same, never wanting to do anything. You never see the vision that we have. I think there is something wrong with your beliefs in Allah."

The doctor sat down, staring in shock and praying that when he was let go, he'd be able to find a sanctuary for himself and his children. He wanted to immediately begin a search for a cure. He knew if the time allowed it, he would have a chance. But he didn't believe that Imad was a man of patience, nor that he would wait that long to release this death on America.

Imad selected a chair and sat in it. He motioned with a rolling finger and the man behind the camera smiled. Imad said, "Good evening, ladies and gentleman of America and across the world. My name is Imad and I am the leader of the organization named Allah's Hand. We were sent here, to your country, to help with the infestation of filth and scum. We are here to help cleanse your country. You will thank us, if your God allows you into the heaven that you believe in. The disease that we have cannot be stopped. It cannot be cured, and you will have no chance of escaping it. It will travel faster than anything you could ever imagine. I hope that in your next life, you can avoid the sins that you will pay for today."

The cameraman gave a thumbs up, then down when he saw a message that he did not understand flashing on the message system. "I do not know what this is saying, Imad. I do not know if we were able to get what you wanted."

Imad rose to his feet and looked at the message. "The battery is low, you son of a whore." He let out a short breath. "You would die if we were home. You know that, do you not, Mohammed?"

The man nodded his head. "Yes, and I would be deserving of it as well, Imad. A thousand apologies to you, Imad. I am very sorry. I will learn how to use it before we attack Europe."

Imad smiled, nodding his head slowly. "We will be making a lot of these videos, and I will need you to learn your jobs. I will need all of you to learn your damn jobs."

The men nodded, watching the people in the room. Their faces were turning blotchy and red rashes were spreading on their skin. Imad yelled, "How long does this take to work?"

The doctor got up from his chair and approached the window slowly. He stared at the hostages, watching their eyes. He turned around, knowing that he would be going to hell for what he had done here. "It has started. Their skin will turn red, followed by rashes and sores. They will get a fever and go into convulsions. Then their brains will spasm and they will die."

"Yes, but how long do they have left before they are free from their sin?"

The doctor stared, single tears at first followed by

many more making their way down his dark cheeks. He stared through the two-sided mirror, thinking of his children and wondering if he had made the right choice. He wasn't even confident that Imad would free him when he saw the end results of his modified disease. He placed his palm to the mirror, wishing to reach out and cure them. He smiled, thinking about his wife and found her voice in the back of his head, telling him that he was going to find a way to resolve the problem and that he would not be punished for what he had done. He was going to be forgiven by Allah because he was doing right by his family. Imad saw him smiling and took it wrong. He pointed at the doctor, yelling to his men, "Would you look at the humanitarian doctor! He is finally showing he has something between his legs. He likes it. Now, doctor, how long until the effects take place?"

He stopped smiling as he looked up at all of the men, so proud of themselves and none feeling any remorse about the horrible things that they had just done. He stared for a moment at Imad and then looked back at the hostages. He looked down at his chart and realized that it was working much faster than he had expected it to. He looked up. "It is supposed to take days, but it appears to be taking effect much quicker than intended."

Imad looked through the window, a smile from ear to ear and clapped his hands in pure delight. He could not have been more pleased by this news. "How long do you think until they are completely taken out by the virus, doctor? I thought original plans would be weeks."

Doctor Abul turned around, shrugging. "Did you want me to take a few more weeks with the research? I might able to make the incubation period in people go longer. If they live longer, they would suffer more. If you just let me know what you want, it is my desire to obey. You know that I will do anything at this point to get my children back."

Imad held up his hands yelling loudly. "No! Don't do anything stupid, doctor! If they can die quicker, that is best.

We will have to spread it through the nation so it will fall faster than expected. This is good news, not bad."

After a few hours, they watched the people, no longer upright but resting against the walls. They were covered with sweat, their clothes damp from it, and the men had unbuttoned their once crisp dress shirts. Imad was walking on clouds at this point. His every plan was coming to fruition. He knew if his father could see what was happening, he would be in awe that America would finally be taken to its knees. He packed the briefcase with the contents of the disease. They had divided them into fifteen different containers, each one rigged with a timer. When the timers went off, the virus would be sent into the airways spreading it everywhere, turning the deadly liquid into an even more deadly gas form.

Dr. Abul looked at the briefcase and asked, "You have many containers there, Imad. What do you plan to do with all of them?"

"Very simple. We will be going across America; we will be going to the largest corporations in New York, California, Boston, Texas, Florida, and others. Not only will America fall but its economy will as well. If there is no one able to do the work, the stock market will crash it will be a thing of pure beauty."

The doctor sat on the edge of the desk thinking about it all. He looked up nodding, "Imad, that is actually genius. You would cripple everything associated to America. People would not be allowed to get assistance from America. The countries that relied on them as a crutch no longer would be able to stand and would also fall."

Imad's men smiled, proudly knowing in their hearts that they would be with Allah one day and treated as kings. Imad gave each of the men a quick embrace. Mohammed was the only one to go with him. As they were leaving, one of the men asked, "What about the doctor and his children, sir? What do you want us to do about them?"

Imad smiled, looking at the man, staring at him

because his life depended on it. "We do not want him coming up with a cure, even if it would not be immediate. When these people die, I want you to kill them all. You can give him a dose of his own drug, but I do not want anything happening to the family until we know that it will work."

Doctor Abul said, "But you told me that if and when I was able to do what you asked, you would let us go. Do you have no honor? Do you believe in nothing?"

Imad shrugged, "I owe you nothing. You are no better than one of them. It would seem by the looks of the patients that you have hours left to live, at best. Let him have a moment with his children before you give them all the drug. I don't want anyone saying that I do not have a heart."

The four men staying laughed at this as Imad and Mohammed left to go on their chosen path.

*****

Jonathan saw what Gabriel was talking about and set the helicopter down on the opposite end of a field. He hadn't needed Gabriel to point out the obvious and tell him that he should take the giant craft behind a bed of trees to land. Gabriel had barely let the chopper set down when he was already sliding the door open.

Jonathan knew what he had to do and disliked the thought of drawing gunfire or attention, but at the same time, knew that if this unthinkable drug came to fruition and spread, there would be little he could do to save his own son. He stared at Gabriel for a moment, thinking that he was most likely America's last hope. He knew there would be nothing bullets could do to fight the evil that they had created in that building.

Gabriel got out and handed Jonathan one of the walkie-talkies he'd taken. "Stay on channel three. If you're alive when we get out of this, then I might need a ride. We don't know if they are even still there."

"I'll be all right. I'm going to go out for a half hour and come back in buzzing the building. It should give you plenty of time to make it in there. Is there anything else that I can do for you? Do you need me to do anything to help besides that?"

Gabriel handed him a backpack. "Toss this out your window near the building. I took it from the armory when I was gearing up. You pull this string here and you make sure that you are not anywhere in the vicinity when it goes off."

"It's a bomb, isn't it? How long do I have before it goes off?"

"Twenty seconds maybe. I'd let it go and get the fuck out of dodge once you pull that. If there is one thing about the CIA, it's that just because it has an ETA on detonation, that doesn't mean anything when it comes to when the damn thing will actually go off.

Jonathan nodded. "Don't worry. I won't keep this thing any longer than I need to. Once you get the place secured, you let me know and I can get reinforcements to back you up if you need it."

Gabriel shook his head. "You make sure that you get a medical team ready. There will be people who are going to need help if they're doing human experiments in there."

Jonathan said, "No, I meant if you need backup with the terrorists.

Gabriel said, "They will never know I'm coming."

Gabriel closed the door, twirling his finger to let him know to take off. Jonathan watched his gauges, making sure that he was set. When he looked back out, Gabriel had already disappeared into the woods. Gabriel had waited for him to take off and had sprinted across the field to the tunnel where the plant's waste was sent out. Gabriel slipped on a hazardous waste mask, glad that he was going into an American waste tunnel and not a third world country, where the fluids coming out could cause him sure death. He ducked, running quickly through it. He had seen nothing but a few rats in the tunnel. When he came up into the building, he kept a watchful gaze. He heard the machines running that powered the building, boilers running full bore. He walked slowly and carefully, but after a few minutes, he realized that there was very little staff in the building. He had not seen or heard anyone yet. He walked through the basement, prying a map of the building off the wall. He saw the security room on the map and made his way there first. When he came to the room, he heard music blaring and looked inside.

He saw an Iranian man sitting behind the tower of computer monitors that had almost every inch of the building under surveillance. Gabriel was glad that this man hadn't been putting a lot of effort into his assignment; he had made it this far into the building undetected. He scratched on the door and a man yelled, "What do you want? It is not locked!"

Gabriel said nothing, he just tapped on the door again, and after a moment, the man got up, cursing aloud as he walked to the door. He opened it up with his gun still slung on his shoulder, a fresh cigarette sitting between his lips. "I said what do you want?"

Gabriel pulled the man out by the front of his collar and gripped his rifle from behind him, twisting the strap repeatedly until it was strangling the man. Gabriel slammed the man back into the security room hard. He tried everything he could to get Gabriel to let go, but it was useless, and after a minute, the man started to fall to his knees. He had never stopped twisting the rifle, and the man's face was near purple by the time he'd finally taken his last breath. Gabriel let the man down easy, dragging him to the back of the office, knowing by the time he was found, it would be too late for any of them.

Gabriel searched through the rooms, seeing that the company left very little to the imagination. They did not believe in their employees' honesty, as he found that every room was wired. He scrolled through, finding one filled with a man and three small children. He pulled out his file, skimming it and coming to the section detailing the doctor. He saw a picture of him with his family noted in there as well. The children in the picture looked younger and smaller. He saw no wife in the picture and as he read further, he saw that she had been found dead in the family's home.

Gabriel finished scrolling through the footage, seeing only five men. Four were in the office holding the doctor and one man was guarding the children. He saw the parking lot in one shot and hit the rewind function on it. It showed two men a few hours ago, heading out to a large SUV, wheeling something behind them. He tried his radio to let Jonathan know to contact in, but had no signal this deep in the basement. He went back further seeing everyone in the office leaving at once and realized it was just the normal time that a regular person left work.

He watched as the man with the children was talking on his radio. He pulled out his pistol and made sure that he had one in the chamber. The man ushered the children out into the hall and the four of them headed towards the office. Gabriel was confident that he knew what was about to happen and left the security room in a sprint. He peered at the map of the building as he made his way to where they were. Gabriel made it in between him and the office that they were heading to and waited patiently, catching his breath.

When the man crossed the doorway, Gabriel reached out from the darkness and pulled the man back into the darkness with him. The man tried to scream, but Gabriel cupped his mouth as he slid the knife into his lung. The man elbowed at Gabriel and as he did, Gabriel gripped his arm, raising it up and slid the knife in the arteries of his armpit, turning the blade and bringing it down his side. The man screamed in pain behind Gabriel's hand and Gabriel delivered one final blow to the man's neck. He took the momentum going down his side and transferred it into an upward motion, jamming the knife up into the man's neck; his eyes bulged as the knife pierced. The man's legs went out from beneath him and Gabriel let him fall to the floor.

Gabriel put his fingers on his face, feeling nothing but

the man's blood. Not wanting to frighten the kids, he wiped it off. He moved to the hallway and found the three faces all looking numb. They didn't look like they had seen anything that resembled love in a very long time. He knelt down in front of them, not wanting to assume. He asked, "Do you speak English?"

The oldest of the three looked at Gabriel, his eyes filled with fear. Gabriel patted the boy on the shoulder. "It's okay if you speak. You are safe now, I promise you."

The youngest whispered, "We speak English. That man is mean. He does not let us talk."

Gabriel nodded. "Well, I took care of him and he won't hurt you again, I can promise you that. Have you seen your father recently?"

The children shook their heads slowly; the oldest spoke, "We have not seen him in a very long time. These men came to our home and broke in. They killed our mother and took us on a very long trip. We have been kept in this place for as long as I can remember. We don't know if our father is even alive."

Gabriel stood, looking around and motioned for the children to follow him. "Your father is safe and alive. I'm going to take you somewhere to hide. Do you think that you can do that for me? If you can stay in one place, I will get your dad and then the four of you can go somewhere safe."

The youngest asked, "Is there such a place away from them?"

Gabriel never stopped walking. "There will be no one left to harm you after today."

They went through the halls slowly, the children mimicking his walk and trying to keep up with his long legs. When Gabriel found a break room, he ushered them in, setting them up with drinks and snacks. All of them looking like they could use a month or two of healthy meals. Their clothes were too short on their legs and too tight for their waists, and all of them worn and dingy; it appeared that they had not been allowed to change them very often. The children saw the food and attacked it. Gabriel said, "You stay here. Don't leave and I will be back with your dad."

The little one gave a thumbs up, stuffing a package of cookies into his face. He smiled and Gabriel thought it might have been the first time he had done so since he had been taken and his mother murdered. He shut the door slowly and quietly, then went back to the dead man and stripped his radio off of his belt. The radio was going off with screams from his men who had been obviously waiting for him to come with the children. Gabriel answered, "I am on my way; one of the little bastards had to take a shit."

The voice said, "Well, why didn't you answer before?"

Gabriel barked back at him, "Who are you, my mother? What the hell hurry are you in? We will be there soon."

"We can leave once we give the disease to them. I am ready to leave and go home finally."

"We are all ready to go home, brother."

"Just hurry up," the man said.

Gabriel made his way down the hall to the wing where the doctor was being held. He walked slowly, peering into the room that the hostages were in, noticing that they were lying on the floor, not moving. He stared at the group while watching their chests. After a few minutes, he could just barely see the faintest of movement rising and falling, telling him that they weren't lost yet. He knocked on the door and waited for the handle to twist. When it did, Gabriel slammed a foot into it. The man on the other end had his nose caught by the edge of the door, breaking it and covering his front with blood. Gabriel moved in through the doorway. The man with the broken nose stood just inside, doubled over in pain. Gabriel brought a boot straight up at the man's head. The force of the kick propelled him back onto a table. The man left in charge cowered behind the doctor who held up his hands, eyes shut. The doctor was sure that his life was over.

Gabriel aimed at the other two men, firing twice into each heart to make sure they would no longer be a threat.

The man in charge screamed, "If you do not put your gun down, I will shoot him in the head! Do you hear me? I swear to you, I will shoot him!"

Gabriel looked at the doctor and then back at the terrorist. "Who is this man? Is he important?"

The man looked at Gabriel curiously, "If you are not here for him, then why are you here?"

"Didn't you hear?"

"Hear what?"

"There's an abundance of assholes here." Gabriel fired the pistol once, leaving a new hole in the man's forehead. The force of the bullet snapped his neck back and he crashed into the wall. A single stream of blood wound down his forehead from the hole. The man slid to the ground leaving a blood trail down the side of the office wall.

Gabriel looked at the doctor, realizing he, too, looked like a skeleton, just barely standing on his own feet. Gabriel pointed the gun at the man. "What is your name? Who are you?"

He looked at Gabriel, raising his hands slowly, unsure who the hell he was or that he was here to help. "My name is Dr. Akbar Abul. I have been held here for many months. These men have kidnapped my children and murdered my wife. They are bastards."

Gabriel lowered the pistol, looking at the three men, and Abul lowered his hands as well. The man who had been kicked in the face just seconds before was starting to come around. Gabriel raised the pistol, but the doctor walked straight in front of him and grabbed a laptop, gripping it with both hands; as the terrorist began to sit up, the doctor brought it back in an awkward baseball stance and swung the computer, putting everything that he had into it. The man's nose, already looking bad, was now indescribable. The snapping sound that his nose made this time was gut wrenching. Gabriel winced, thinking of the pain the man was going to be feeling if he survived this day. Gabriel asked, "You feel better now?"

The doctor looked at the blood-covered laptop, nodding his head and breathing very heavily. He brought the laptop up over his head again and smashed it into the man's face once and then again. The man's legs shook, and on the third swing, Gabriel stepped forward, gripping the doctor's arm. "That's enough, doctor, please stop."

"You sympathize with this piece of shit? He is a disease; he does not deserve to live, and I pray that he burns in hell for eternity."

Gabriel looked down at the man who was trying to regain his composure and not pass out. He gripped Gabriel's arm limply. Gabriel, staring at the doctor said, "I do not feel for these men, but as of now there is no one to interrogate if this man is killed. Who is left to answer my questions?"

The doctor nodded slowly. "So, we need to keep him alive?"

Gabriel nodded. "It doesn't mean he needs to be happy, though." He gripped the man's wrist, twisting it hard and bending it backwards until he heard it break.

The man screamed in pain and the doctor pointed at him. "His name is Jahid. I almost never get to see him. They have remedial jobs around the plant that they do. They tell me my children are still alive, but I don't have any proof of that."

Gabriel looked at the man, seeing the worry. "I have your children already. They are safe… hungry and undernourished, but they are safe and that's as important as anything, isn't it?"

The doctor clasped his hands together, thanking his God. He looked at Gabriel for a moment, seeing the knives, the pistols, and grenades strapped onto his body. "Who are you, sir? Why are you here?"

"I was hired to free you and your kids, and to take out Imad and his men before they became a threat."

Akbar nodded. "Are they still here? Can I see them?"

Gabriel looked at the observation room. "Did you do this to them? Was that your doing, by chance?"

"Can we speak in private for a minute, please? Do you have something that you can use to restrain him with, please?"

Gabriel flipped the pistol over in his hand, lifted it high in the air, and brought it down with force, pistol-whipping the man. His screaming stopped instantly. He no longer was clutching his wrist, trying to stop the bleeding from the bone that had broken through his dark skin. Gabriel asked, "What is it? If it's important, I need to know. Does it have something to do with the people inside that room?"

The doctor stared at them, nodding. "It has everything to do with them. I have spent the last year of my life dealing with this, day after day. He would not let me leave until I completed his mission. He held the threat of my children's death and my own over my head until he got what he wanted."

Gabriel asked, "So, you are saying that you did what he asked you to?"

"I had no choice. But he knew nothing about what it was that I do. He had an idea, he had a plan, and that was all he could focus on."

Gabriel thought he understood what he was saying, but didn't want to assume anything. "Spell it out. There is a strong chance men more powerful than I am are going to be asking questions and I'm going to need answers."

The doctor looked into the observation room and realized what Gabriel's assumptions were. He put up his hands, trying to keep the stranger calm. "They are fine, sir."

Gabriel couldn't take his eyes off of them, lying on the floor curled in balls; those that were still awake were shivering. The ones who had transitioned into a coma-like state looked as if they were close to the brink of death. "Yeah, they look fucking great. If I go in there, am I going to die?"

The doctor laughed, which Gabriel took as mockery and an insult. He gripped the doctor and swung him in the air, lifting him off of his feet, and slammed him up against the window hard enough to make it shake. The doctor grunted as the air was knocked out of his lungs. Gabriel screamed, "You think this is funny? Do you have any fucking idea what these men were going to do? You do realize that when they were done with you, you and your family would be dead, right? I just saved your ass and now you think this is funny? How about I throw you in there with them? Would that be funny to you then?" Gabriel let him down and pulled his knife from its sheath and placed it up against his thin neck. "Do you think this would be funny? If I just push it in one inch, you die. Did you not want to see your kids again?"

The doctor took in a long deep breath, trying to stay calm. He whispered, scared to have his neck twitch for fear that he would be dead if he did. "You misunderstand me, sir. I do not want anything to happen to you or to the people of America. If you lower the knife I can explain." Gabriel nodded and pulled the knife back. He released the grip on the man's shirt, patting him on the chest and trying to remain cool. The doctor cleared his throat. "I did what he asked, but I thought once he knew I had made what he wanted, he would leave and be in too big a rush to stick around and see what happened with the disease."

"What are you trying to say? Get to it because you are saying he already left with the disease."

"Those men and women are in terrible pain. They would rather be dead right now than wait, and that is only speaking for those not sleeping."

"Wait for what?"

"For it to pass, of course. I took a strain of the flu and made a hybrid strain. It makes two-week flu symptoms: fevers, shakes, sweats, and coma, all in a matter of forty-eight hours. It would cripple America, but that would only be for a few days."

Gabriel looked at the hostages. "So, you are saying that they will only have this for a few days? What took you a year to do it then?"

The doctor stared. "I wanted to make sure they lived. It took a year to make sure it would act like a deadly virus while not having the same result. I could never do that even if it meant the death of my children and myself. I knew in my heart that I was doing the right thing. But I fear now that Imad might do something ignorant."

"Why do you think he will change his plans now that he has what he finally wants? Don't you think he will keep on target going forward?"

"Not when he finds out about his men, he won't; he will deviate from it and God knows what he will do. If he follows the path of his father, he will probably resort back to bombs... especially if they find out about this being a hybrid flu."

Gabriel stared at the people lying in the room and said, "They need to die. You and your children need to die. It needs to be public, or they won't come out from the shadows."

The doctor was confused as he gripped Gabriel's chest crying, "I've been through too much to have you come along and kill us. We can disappear. We can leave and never be found again."

Gabriel nodded. "I am going to make some phone calls. These men will erase any existence of you being alive. By the time I make these phone calls, you'll be dead, but you won't feel a thing, I promise. Gabriel handed him a pistol and said, "Now keep an eye on that man in there. If he wakes up go ahead and shoot him. But remember, we do need him for a little bit longer."

The doctor asked, "What are you going to do?"

"I'm going to go and get your kids. You do want to see them, don't you?"

The man was quick for a little guy; he lunged at

Gabriel and embraced him in a hug. "Let go of me now. I will go get your kids. I'm sure that they're more appreciative of your hugs than I am."

The man slapped his forehead. "I'm sorry. I owe you my life and I don't even know your name yet. I apologize. It's just that all of this is a bit overwhelming."

He held out a hand, not having met anyone new in quite a while. "My name is Gabriel. I am honored to meet you. It was a rare thing that you did. Many would not have."

The men shook firmly, and the doctor said, "You do know that I will forever be in your debt."

Gabriel walked out the door. "You just stay here. Don't go running away and I'll be back with your kids in a few minutes."

Gabriel headed into the break room. The children were sitting around the table with a mountain of wrappers in front of them. They sat back, each with messy smiles on their faces. They snapped to attention when Gabriel entered. When he saw this, he realized it might take time for them to learn what normal was again. He knelt down in front of them and said, "Hey, I found your dad. Do any of you kids want to go see him?"

The three kids looked at each other anxiously, shooting their hands into the air and waving them. Gabriel smiled, rubbing the youngest child's hair. "Let's go surprise your dad. He's going to be very happy to see you. Don't worry. We're going to find somewhere comfortable and safe with all the food that you can eat anytime you want. Your life has just begun."

They walked back down the hall quickly. Gabriel was not worried about the threats but knew that even the CIA was going to need some time to try to pull off the idea that he had in mind. He went back to the office and entered, motioning for Dr. Abul to come outside of the room. As the doctor started to approach, Gabriel pointed to his right hand. The doctor looked down, and Gabriel nodded. Akbar placed it on the table and brought up a shaking hand. He walked in a daze, not believing that he and his family were safe, even if he did not understand all of the details behind it yet. He only cared that he had his children with him. Gabriel pushed the door all the way open, and the broken man saw his three children; they all were a little taller and skinnier. He saw his wife smiling at him in their faces and he rushed towards them, bending down and taking the three of them into his arms. He twirled them around in a circle, kissing each one of them on the forehead over and over.

Gabriel looked down at the kids and he said, "Do you think you can take your dad back to the break room for me? Between you and me, he looks hungry. Why don't you go get him something to eat and drink?"

The little one gave a quick thumbs up and winked before pulling his father down the hall by the hand. Akbar asked, "Will you come for me when you are done? Will I see you again?"

Gabriel said, "I can't answer that just yet, but you and your family will be safe. I can at least promise you that much."

The doctor nodded, smiling. "Be careful, Gabriel. We can't always be lucky enough to have angels watching out for us."

Gabriel closed the door as he took in the terrorist still lying on the table, unconscious. "I pray for the angels' sake that they are not watching me."

The family walked down the hall, enjoying every moment of being together again. The fact that they were reunited felt like a gift from God himself. They did as Gabriel asked and went to the break room where the doctor checked his children, making sure that they were physically okay.

Gabriel walked up, slapping the man in the face as the fat on his cheek jiggled. When he didn't wake, Gabriel slapped him again and again until he started to come back to life. He looked up, and saw Gabriel standing in a shadow of the room. He tried to sit up, forgetting about his broken wrist and screamed at the top of his lungs, using words that Gabriel could barely understand. He protected the hand, setting it on his chest and pushing up with his other hand. As he did so, the pain from his ruined nose slammed him, taking his breath away for a moment. He glared at Gabriel through watering eyes. "Who the fuck are you?"

"I'm the good guy. I need to know where Imad and Mohammed went."

The man laughed, making one of his last mistakes. "You cannot do anything to me; you are American government, no? You must take me to jail, give me lawyer, feed, clothe me, and get me a doctor for my wounds. Get me my rights, you monkey! Go now!"

Gabriel leaned into the light, his dark eyes burning with rage. "Let me explain just a little something about who I am." He raised his pistol, firing one shot into the man's right kneecap. The pain was excruciating and the man screamed until his vocal cords gave out. Gabriel walked up to the man, laid out magazines for his pistol, and said, "You don't think I can do this all night? I will cut every inch of skin off of your body, one piece at a time."

The man held up his hands towards Gabriel and began to beg. Gabriel smacked them away and fired a second shot into his other knee. The man screamed again. "You didn't even ask me a question! Why did you shoot me?"

"I wanted to make sure you understood that I was serious. You living is not a priority to me. It's really not important at all. If you give me any reason to doubt you, the pain will only increase."

The man nodded, tears streaming from his blood-soaked face. Fresh sweat gleamed across his forehead. "I don't know what I can tell you that you don't know already."

"Assume that I know nothing. If I run out of places to put bullets, I'll find new ways to make sure you feel the pain. Tell me now if you have questions or forever hold your peace."

"Like I say, I do not think that you know much less than—"

Gabriel took his thumb and dug it into the man's fresh gunshot wound on his knee. He tried to scream aloud, but Gabriel punched him in the stomach, making the man puke every bit of the last meal that he had consumed. Gabriel let him finish and, when he was done, grabbed him by his greasy, unwashed, black hair and screamed, "Tell me where Imad is now!"

The man looked up to the ceiling. "Oh I beg you, Allah, please take me now! I am not strong enough to handle this."

Gabriel pulled his eyes back down to meet his and yelled, "You pray to me to kill you! Because I am the only one that will grant you an end." He punched the man again, this time bringing a fresh onslaught of blood. "Tell me where Imad is, and do it now!"

The man held up both hands, coughing out mucus. "Please… please do not hurt me anymore. I swear to you, I will talk. I will talk; do not punish me."

Gabriel leaned in, whispering in his ear, "I have not even started punishing you. This is only interrogation."

His screams filled the hallway and when he was done, Gabriel's hands were both soaked in blood. He stared at them, knowing that he had gone past what he should have. At the same time, a thousand years of punishment would not make up for the pain that he deserved to endure.

Gabriel left the man on the table when he went to look for a phone. He knew that there was nothing left of the man to worry about. If he lived another five minutes, he wouldn't make it ten feet from where he lay bleeding. When he found a phone, he called the private number and asked for Frank. "Gabriel? I have Tony with me. Did you succeed?"

"I have the doctor and his family. They could use a good meal but they are—"

"I didn't ask for a health report on the family. I asked *did you accomplish your mission*? Are you in control of the disease? Are we going to be able to divert the worst case?"

"I found the doctor, but Imad and his second in command, Mohammed, both escaped before I got here. There was nothing I could have done to get them."

"God damn it, Gabriel! You don't call me and tell me that you only did half of your mission! Fuck, Tony, I thought you said this guy was reliable, damn it!"

Tony coughed and Gabriel figured he was probably chain-smoking at this point. "Gabriel is the most reliable agent we've ever had. If you sent him in a day late and a dollar short, what the fuck did you expect him to do?"

"Well, at least tell me that you got the disease covered Gabriel? Throw a little fucking light on the situation!

"He took the modified disease strain with him as well but—"

Frank screamed, "You've got to be fucking kidding me! What, what the hell did you even do, goddammit?"

"Frank?"

"What?"

"I need you to stop talking… I want you to wire my money back into my account and then I need you to do the following steps."

"Who do you think is in charge here?"

"I am. Because I have the doctor and knowledge; you haven't shut up long enough to hear me. There needs to be a news announcement stating that everyone died including the doctor, the kids, Imad's men, and the hostages that they were doing experiments on."

"Wait! They are doing human trials already? We can't just lie to the media. What if they look into it? What do we do then? What about the victims' families? What do we tell them?"

"You swoop in, get their families, and let them know what is happening. These people are going to need to be quarantined for a month to be sure they are really okay, anyway. The people were infected, but the doctor made a super strain of the flu virus. The people went through hell, but the doctor, for the greater good of the world, made the drug non-life-threatening. It will not take out everyone in the country. It only has a shelf life of a few days; it can still cripple the nation, but it won't kill us if it does make it out. That doctor is a hero for not letting this get out into the open. He could have been finished months ago with the project if he had just wanted everyone dead. He risked the lives of himself and his family to keep that outbreak from becoming a killer."

"So, how do we get Imad? What plan do you have?"

Tony cut in, "Hey Gabriel, we will make the calls and get it arranged. We will do the heavy lifting. Can I trust that you have a plan here for the next step to get Imad? Are you going to be able to recover the disease?"

"Just make sure you do it. You'll know when it's taken care of. Frank, make sure my money is put back."

"We aren't doing a thing until you come in and—"

"I won't be coming in again. If you give me reason to come in, you are going to have issues, Frank."

"Until I see you again, you won't have a dime to your name, Gabriel."

"If that's the way you want it. You'll know when it's done, though. You can call Jonathan and tell him not to drop that bomb; it isn't going to be needed." Gabriel looked at his watch. "You might want to call him pretty quickly. He's going to be coming in soon, ready to blow it up."

"You come in when this is over, Gabriel," Frank said.

Gabriel ended the call and disappeared as the CDC and CIA joint efforts came in, ready to tell people about the outbreak. When the staff came in and saw the terrorists, there was no doubt a pro hitter had been there. All of them were curious about who it would have been, knowing they didn't use men like that anymore.

Chapter 10
Imad

Imad sat in the large hotel room, staring at the container and smoking a cigarette. He had been watching news updates constantly for a week now, gleefully happy that America was in a state of panic. He knew there was no chance they could do anything to save themselves, but they were trying to reassure Americans that they were safe. Imad yelled, "Hey Mohammed! Did you hear what that blonde bitch was saying on the news? They claim they have it on good account that the two terrorists still at large have fled the country—that they have abandoned the cause and are on their way back to the caves in Iran. Can you believe this shit?"

Imad rose to his feet when Mohammed did not answer. He moved into the kitchen area and saw him sitting at the table, facing away. "Are you deaf, Mohammed? Did you hear what I said? They are running for their lives. They do not have any plans because they have too many people and there is no way to save them all. The President is in hiding. This is wonderful, and we have not even had to release the first of the bombs yet."

He looked at the open window then at Mohammed. He walked slowly to his friend and placed a hand on his shoulder. When he shook him a little, his friend fell to the side; his eyes were still open, but he was long dead. Imad jumped back a foot, sucking in air. He looked down at Mohammed, seeing the dark blood in contrast to his pressed white shirt. His neck had been slit from ear to ear. Blood covered his front and he had a strip of black tape across his mouth. Imad whispered, "Mohammed, no."

Gabriel walked out of the side room, pistol raised as he stared Imad in the eyes. "Hello, Imad. You've been a true pain in the ass. You broke my first rule by killing the wife. Then you starved children for an entire year."

Imad screamed, "Your people have—"

Gabriel shot him in the knee. "I have no people. I work alone."

Imad screamed as the pain became immense. "You shot me! What do you want from me?"

"I want you to hate every minute of your life until the last one comes."

Gabriel shot him in the other knee. Imad sat up, trying to pull himself backwards, his bloody legs leaving a trail on the floor. Gabriel shot one of his hands, and when Imad screamed again, he shot him in the other had. "What do you want, damn it?"

Gabriel, never so much as losing his temper, said, "I want you to be an example for others... others who think that they can come to my country and try to strike fear in our hearts."

Gabriel leveled the gun again, shooting him in one thigh and then the other thigh. Imad screamed, "Kill me, you son of a bitch! Fucking kill me now!"

Gabriel shot the man in both arms, knelt down in front of him, and looked at the blood as it flowed. Imad started to nod his head forward, trying to let himself pass out. Gabriel slapped him hard, with an open hand, waking him up quickly. Imad said, "Why won't you just kill me? Why won't you put me out of my misery?"

Gabriel slid the gun back into its holster with a smile and pulled a scalpel from a case he carried. He carved a message into the man's chest after nailing his hands to the wall. *"My name is not important. Your beliefs mean nothing to me. There are no laws that govern me, which will save you. There is nowhere you can hide that will keep me from you. Jurisdiction means nothing to me and I have no handler. Beware G is out there and he watches over all of you."*

Gabriel sat back, staring at the man. "That probably hurt didn't it?"

Imad had run out of tears. He tried to speak, but only blood came from his mouth. He stared in the corner where his

179

tongue lay. He was trying his best to say, "Kill me. Kill me, please. I can suffer no more."

Gabriel smiled as he set the case in front of him and opened it. He leaned in close, making the man jump. "You want to know a secret? The disease in this bag. It's the reason that I've hunted you and set you up for death. It's the reason that you've put many through hell."

Imad nodded. It looked as if it was the last thing he could handle before he passed to another world. A world where he thought he would be rewarded for his sacrifice… where he would be sent to sit alongside his father and men who passed long before him.

Gabriel said, "The reason that it took a year to get the disease to work, the reason he was not done in a few weeks, or in a few months was simple. He never created something that would kill anyone. He worked his ass off month after month to develop something that appeared to kill someone. Something that looked horrible—like hell unleashed. He told this me when I saved him and killed all of your men… much like I have done to you. He would have put his family second and let himself and them die if he was unable to produce what he was trying to make. He would never do something to a country that he thought was so great. I had the news set up all of the reports so that I could track you down. I had to wait for you to make a mistake, allowing me to get into the building and gain access."

Imad shook his head repeatedly. Gabriel took a picture of the children with the doctor and showed it to him. It was the last thing his eyes would ever see, except for the blade cutting them out. He screamed a guttural cry and Gabriel pulled the man's phone from his pocket. He took down his contact information and placed an open call to the CIA. Gabriel said, "Tell Frank Fox that Imad is at the location where this number can be traced."

The agent on the other end said, "Wait! We need more information from you."

"No you don't. Write this down and make sure that you relay it to Frank Fox. Tell him that I got his disease secured, and I got the last two terrorists, and the next time I check my bank accounts that I'd better see every last fucking cent. Now make sure that you are taking this down verbatim. I don't want any question of what my intentions and thoughts are."

"Who is this? Can I tell him that?"

"Just tell him if I don't get my money, he'd better figure out a way to not sleep. Not that it is going to do him any good."

"Sir, it is a crime to threaten another..."

"Did you write down everything I said?"

"Um, yes, I did... and I have you recorded as well."

"Good. I'm glad it's recorded. Just get him that; it will get the point across better. He's a bit on the fucking stupid side, so I'd appreciate leaving as little amount of questions as we can for him. Tony, if you can hear this, you can sleep at night... and if the shit is about to hit the fan, it would seem you have the means and ability to get ahold of me. When America has nowhere else to turn, make the call and I'll be there."

The line on the other end was silent. Eventually, the lady cleared her throat and asked, "Who the hell are you?"

Gabriel set the phone down on his end, and the woman could only hear the whimpering of Imad. Gabriel picked up Mohammed's phone and called the news station. When a man answered, Gabriel said, "If you want a breaking news story— and you don't want to miss out on this one—then you need to come to 562 Leeland York Street."

"What's the rush, buddy?"

"If you don't get here in a few minutes, the CIA is going to beat you to it and they are going to lock this fucker down. You aren't going to have any chance at seeing it or getting the inside story. There are no second chances today; you either make it or you don't."

"Did you say the CIA? You mean the Central Intelligence—"

Gabriel cut in, "If you don't move now, it is already going to be too late. They will never disclose any of this. Stop wasting time or you are going to have to explain to your boss how you missed the biggest story of the year."

"Yeah, yeah… you are right, buddy. Thanks. You are a damn saint, man."

Gabriel laughed into the phone as he stared at the dismembered terrorists lying in front of him. "Yeah, I'm just a regular fucking angel. Get moving now."

Epilogue

Frank sat across from Tony, who was smoking a cigarette, as they tried to write up a report. A knock at the door interrupted them and a secretary poked her head in. "Mr. Fox, I have a message for you. I think that you are going to want to see this, sir."

Frank looked up. He was sick of trying to make a report that would work for everyone. He did not yet know how he was going to explain that the man they hired to save the doctor was the same man who killed a high-level protected witness. He motioned for her to come in with his fingers. She pushed through the door, bringing a laptop and a typed manuscript. Frank said, more joking than anything, "Thank you, Veronica. I appreciate you taking the time to drop that off. Do you think it is a priority?"

She looked at the papers and back up at the two men. "If I were you, sir, I'd fix whatever it was you did with this guy's money and set it straight, with interest."

He held his hand up reading it and then the two listened to the recording on the laptop. Frank looked more perturbed than nervous. "What do you think, Tony?"

Tony sat back in his seat, kicking his feet up and smiling. After the last few days, he'd given up any worries about smoking in a federal building and lit up another of what seemed like an endless chain-smoking marathon. "What do you mean what do I think? I think it's fucking great! Did you hear the thing at the end? He told me that I was safe to sleep! That is as good as gold. If Gabriel says it, he means it. The idea that I don't have to worry about him... do you know how great that is?"

Frank smiled, not putting a lot of compassion into it. "I can't tell you how happy I am that you are going to be okay, Tony. Really, that reassures me and I feel so happy. You know that he can't touch us. He'd have everyone in the country after him if he tried taking one of us out. You think

183

he knows that?"

"My concern with Gabriel isn't whether he understands. The problem with Gabriel is that he doesn't give a shit. If you don't fix this, he's going to come after you. Do you want to put your wife through something like that?"

"She's tough. Besides, I thought that Gabriel has that moral code that keeps him from hurting a woman or children?"

"That has nothing to do with that. It's what he will do to you in front of her. If you are lucky, he might make it so you only need to drink from a straw for the rest of your life."

"And this is the guy that you want to rely on when the shit hits the fan and the nation is at its worst?"

"Yep, it might not be pretty, but he gets it done. He might do some things that we don't like, but I'll be damned if he doesn't come through. He'd probably still be working for us if we hadn't screwed him over in South America all those years ago. It wasn't his fault we couldn't get him out. You going to give him his money back?"

"How do I explain something like that to the accountants?"

Tony shrugged. "It wasn't my idea in the first place. You fucked the pooch on that. I told you we could have thought of something else to get him to take the job. You said we needed to use money, because you didn't understand Gabriel. You didn't listen, and now you have the devil on your heels and you still don't seem to appreciate the circumstances that are hovering behind you."

Frank opened his mouth to speak, but Veronica came back in unannounced. "I'm sorry to interrupt, but I think that the two of you need to see this."

Frank, who was finally starting to worry about his longevity on Earth tried to get her to leave. "Veronica, you can't just barge in here. This is classified."

"I can appreciate that, sir. You know that I would not barge in, but I think that you might want to see what is happening on the news. It is blowing up on all the local stations."

She hit the television, and they saw a blonde-haired news reporter outside, trying to use the grimmest face that she had to show her concern for the men in the hotel room behind her. She was clueless as to who the two men were and kept referring to them as victims. The camera panned to her right and zoomed in on a blood-covered man, showing a message carved into his chest. The camera then panned back out, revealing that the man's eyes and tongue had been removed. Tony stood up and walked to the television. He turned around, pointing at Frank. "You fucking pay him! You figure it out, goddammit. I don't care how, but you make sure Gabriel gets paid. He's going to come after you and then we are both fucked. I know he said that I was okay, but I'll be damned if I'm going to leave something to chance that could just as easily be fixed with a few clicks of a mouse."

Frank saw the man, as well as the message. "Seems like he got a bit patriotic, didn't he? As he looked closer at the television, he hit the pause button and looked through his files, bringing out a picture of Imad and Mohammed. He pointed at it. "He… he got Imad. He did it. There are the containers the doctor told us about. They looked exactly like the ones he described. Holy shit! That crazy bastard said he would find them and he did it. He took care of them so we don't even have to worry about trying the son of a bitch."

Tony was watching the paused screen and he motioned to Veronica. "Hey! Turn that on would you?"

When she did, Tony watched in awe as he saw Imad's lips moving slowly. They were impossible to make out. The blood that covered them mixed with his facial hair and was a black, hairy, bloody mess. Tony pointed at him. "He left the fucker alive, look at him."

Frank said, "It was genius. He lives and he goes to jail a tangled mess. The videos and the interviews will show what happened to him for the rest of his life. Gabriel will force fear into the hearts of terrorists everywhere. They'll think of him as America's personal vigilante. Hell, they'll call him Batman."

Tony grabbed his briefcase. "We can pick this back up in the morning. I can't take any more of this today; you figure out the money and I'll go clean up the news media shit. You have a huge mess to clean up now. If I were you, I would focus on Gabriel's money. Remember his words. He doesn't joke about anything, especially his money."

Frank nodded, looking at Imad and listening to the news reporter finally say, "He looks like he is asking to die. He just wants to die." Seconds later, the cameras were knocked out of the way as police, CIA, and emergency medical techs rushed into the hotel room. The cameras were watching as they pulled the knives from Imad's hands, and he finally fell to the ground.

Frank punched at the keys, furiously looking through his files and trying to do whatever he could to rectify the situation. He found a way at long last to get the money transferred back into Gabriel's account. When he did, he sighed a giant breath of relief, made the sign of the cross, and prayed that it was not too late. He knew also that when he needed to call upon Gabriel again, he would do it under much more respectful terms.

*****

Gabriel drove back to his place. He knew that he needed to stash the truck and then stay on the down low for a good time to come. He looked in the mirror, thinking of Imad, and realized that leaving him alive might be one of the most dangerous moves he had ever made. He thought of the work and the connections a man like that might be able to strike in prison. He also knew it was going to be months before he'd be able to do anything on his own that wasn't from a hospital bed.

Gabriel flipped up his laptop as he pulled over near a Starbucks, knowing he could get a Wi-Fi signal. When he did, he hit the quick link, tapped in his password, and saw that the accounts were back to their normal amounts and, one in particular, had an extra zero in it. He thought of Frank Fox and realized that maybe Tony was able to help him understand why he did not want to aggravate a man like Gabriel.

His phone started to buzz on the dashboard. He hit a button on his steering wheel, muting the music, and pushed the send button on his phone. When he did, a voice came over it before he could speak. "Daddy, it's Mikey. Mommy says we need milk. Are you on your way home yet?"

"Hey buddy. Yeah, Daddy had a long day today. You tell your mom I'll stop and get milk and cookies, okay, Mikey?"

There was a squeal on the other end and then everything went silent. "Jacob, are you still there?"

"Yeah baby. I'll get milk; I just need to wrap up a few more things and then I'll be on my way home, alright?"

"Yeah, I just wanted to tell you how much I love you. There were horrible things happening in the news today and I couldn't stand to think of you being out and about with all this craziness happening. Get home quick, please. I love you."

"Not as much as I love you, baby. I'll see you in a while. Bye for now, honey."

The End
By
Mike Evans

Discover other titles by Mike Evans Visit

The Orphans: Origins

The Orphan: Surviving the Turned
Buried: Broken Oaths

If you have enjoyed Gabriel I would appreciate you taking a minute to go back to Amazon and leave a review, it helps authors immensely!

Gabriel: Only one gets out alive

Overcoming Fear: Molly

By Shaun Phelps

Chapter 1

I'm driving down the road, repeating my new daily routine: "I can do this. I have done this. I will do this. I have lived through this, I will live through this." I repeat the words over and over again until I am just repeating, "I can, I have, I did, I will." I started this routine of positive self-talk about two weeks ago when I first learned I would be teaching substance abuse classes as a part of my mental health internship. I have always had a fear of public speech. Speaking in front of a class of fifteen convicted criminals isn't necessarily public speech but it is somehow just as frightening.

Last week I was told by Dr. Kinsington, my kindly old Professor, that I would be teaching the class by myself. It was fairly convenient of my car to stall, and I regretfully called in to my new workplace to tell them I was broken down and could not make it to work. I did not mention I was only two blocks away. I am ready for my college degree, for sure. I'm just not sure I am ready to confront so many angry people all by myself.

My mentor did reach out to me the next day to make sure my car was working and offered me a ride for this week. It was apparently important to him that I not only attend my internship hours, but also teach his weekly class--as he had other-scheduled sessions that could not be conflicted. I adamantly confirmed my commitment to his program and thanked him again for his belief in me as a student/professional.

So there it is. I can, I have, I did, I will. I know this because I have taught, I was successful and I will be successful again--only before I had my mentor helping me. Tonight I will be alone in a room with a large group of people who wish I was dead. I will survive, I know, because I can, I have, I did, I will.

I show up to the substance abuse center thirty minutes early and begin to review the night's curriculum. Tonight we will be reviewing the downward cycle of substance abuse. How it starts from fun or peer pressure and ends at rock bottom. I will be relying on heart-felt testimony from some of the older members. I can do this. I know I can, because I have, I did, and I will.

I open the doors at fifteen minutes prior to 6 p.m. and start taking roll and money. At 6 p.m. sharp, I lock the door as a part of the state-mandated curriculum of "show up on time or go back to jail." It is a full house tonight. There are fifteen attendees ranging between 18 and 45 years of age. All of them are mirroring an "I want to go the fuck home" look that helps boost my self-esteem.

I start strong, describing how people fall into substance abuse without expecting their lives to fall into complete and utter shit. I draw a downhill slope and ask for examples from the group to show how their life quality had started to decline. After an uncomfortable silence, I describe how people often start keeping secrets from family and start using drugs more frequently than just recreational use. I ask a little more desperately for comments and suggestions and am rewarded with none.

The class ends. I do not die. I narrate the whole hour-and-a-half and avoid any panic attacks. I assign the class homework to analyze how their lives had declined from drug use and send them home at the court-mandated 7:30 p.m.

After the students leave the building, I take a long series of deep breaths, congratulate myself as sincerely as possible on a job well done, and start cleaning the room. As I make my rounds I find some (almost all) of the homework assignments crumpled on the floor or left on or under chairs. My self-esteem is at an all-time high at this point. I'm a failure before I even finish grad school.

After locking up the building, I notice two of my students in the parking lot. A scrawny kid named Steve, the other a kid named Dan equally a runt in size. As I approach them, they lower their eyes and start shuffling in different directions. Steve is in the worst position, as he is standing directly next to his car.

"What's going on, Steve?" I ask politely.

"Nothin' man! Can't a guy just have a polite conversation without being harassed?" Steve responds with an overly defensive tone.

"Dude, seriously? You are selling drugs in my parking lot?" I don't know this for sure but I take a logical leap of faith and give him my best 'for shame' look.

"Man! It's just Molly! It's hardly a drug at all!" Steve starts looking around the parking lot. I'm starting to worry he might be chancing an opportunity to stab me. "Look, man," Steve says nervously, "I don't want any trouble! Please, here, you can have the Molly, I'm coming clean, never doing any drugs again! Your class really taught me a lesson!" Steve shoves a little baggy of crystalized powder into my hand. "Just *please* don't tell my probation officer!"

I stand there for a minute stunned. What the hell just happened? One minute I'm having an innocent conversation and the next minute I'm holding a baggy of glorified Crystal Meth in one hand and the fate of a man in the other. I straighten up to my full 7' stature and give him my best authoritative look. "Just don't let me catch you again."

Steve mutters some gibberish, jumps in his car, and

drives off, leaving me confused and holding an illegal heart attack in a bag.

Holy crap. I'm holding onto illegal drugs! Should I call the police? Should I throw it away? Holy crap! My thoughts spin a mile a minute. I'm not exactly sure why, but instead of throwing it away or calling Steve's probation officer I hide it in the back of my drawer at work, lock the drawer, and the building on my way out.

I drive home in a haze filled with dreary and miserable thoughts. Everything I wish I would have said differently in class, everything I feel I did wrong, and the fact that I left illegal drugs in my desk at work. This has not been a good day.

I park the car and open the door to the sounds of my children, Nivek and Brodie playing. Nivek runs up and gives me a big hug. "Hi, Daddy! Wemissedyousomuch and we'vebeenplayingoutsidealldaybecauseDominiqueis…"

"Heyyyy, buddy, slow down! Dominique is what?" I ask.

"Dominique is sick! Butit'sokayshesaidwecanplayoutside!" We have a gated front yard and we live in a pretty nice community. It isn't unusual for us to let the children play outside. We always have a door or window open so we can listen or keep an eye out for them.

"Oh, well, as long as it's okay! Who is Brodie playing with?" I ask, with an inquisitive look at an elderly man playing catch with my daughter.

"That'sCharleshe'sreallyfunandhejustmovedin!!!" Nivek is a very verbal child, his excitement is infective, but it also tends to make his conversation a bit jumbled. He is eight years old--eleven months older than his eight-year old sister.

He is a handsome and responsible blonde-haired blue-eyed boy who bears no resemblance to his brown-haired brown-eyed father. Brodie, the described sister, is almost an exact image of me, though, with her long, thin brown hair and brown eyes. The only exception is she makes a much prettier girl than I ever could.

"Well, I'm glad Charles is so nice! I will have to talk to him after I check on Dominique!" I then walk past my daughter and Charles and go inside the house to check on Dominique. Something about Charles gives me pause as I open the door. I turn around and see him, a man in his mid-sixties, grey hair, and wrinkles that suggest a lifetime of stories. I notice him sizing me up as well. I don't have grey hair or wrinkles, so I assume he thinks I'm a hippy or a liberal.

"Your name is Charles, right?" I ask without trying to sound defensive.

"'S'right. You the magical Daddy I keep hearin' 'bout?" Charles asks. His southern accent is somewhat disarming, which makes me nervous. But everything makes me nervous--that's why I keep a bottle of Klonopin in my pocket. "Take one milligram four times daily as needed for panic," the bottle sums up my state of mind well.

"I guess that's me. What brings you here, Charles?"

"Oh, I jes' moved to tha area 'n saw yer kids playin' outside, figured I'd come 'n keep 'em some company!" Charles drawls in an enthusiastic way.

"...Well, that's cool, Charles. It's nice to meet you. Thanks for keeping an eye on the kids! I think it's time they come inside for a snack though! Brodie!! Nivek!! Snack time!!!" I yell. It isn't that Charles says anything wrong. I just have a dirty feeling oozing around my skin as he talks. He

195

seems pleasant; I know I am just being paranoid. I'll take some time to talk to him later when I am in a healthier headspace.

After setting the children down to a snack, I walk into the bedroom. The bed is covered in a plush comforter and the only sign of my Dominique is her purple hair sticking out the top.

"Hey babe, how are you feeling?" I ask quietly trying not to startle her.

"I'm fine, I think I just have a stomach bug" she responds with a sleepy voice.

"That's good," I say half listening, "Hey, what's going on with the new guy, Charles? He seems nice but he sort of freaks me out a bit…"

"Aww, Charles is a sweet old man!" Dominique pulls herself up from her bed to give me a *you're being paranoid again* look. "His daughter passed away a few years ago and he just moved here after having heart surgery. Apparently, his wife kicked him out and he's just trying to get a fresh start. He even baked us cookies!"

"Oh my god! Those aren't the cookies I fed the children, are they?!" I get up to run out of the room.

"Charles brought them to me himself, he was so sweet! I tried one and I'm fine." Dominique half stated and half murmured as she laid back down to bed.

Chapter 2

So that's my life: A new week, a new class. I'm starting to get used to the routine. I wake up, shower, freak out, take a pill, keep freaking out, take a consolation pill, freak out while I teach, and freak out all the way home. Each day is falling into a comforting routine, except Charles still bothers me. Every time I get home, he is playing a game with the kids. Nothing to justify my concern, just baseball or catch or badminton; I just can't help the feeling that something is *wrong*. Dominique thinks he's sweet enough. His past tragedy really tugged her heartstrings; who am I to argue with the love of my life? She even invited him over for dinner one night. His thick southern drawl almost had me face-plant into the mashed potatoes.

--

So it's a new day, same routine. I get to my workplace and am startled to see my neighbor, Charles, waiting out front of the building.

"Charles? What brings you here?" I ask with sincere confusion.

"Oh wow! I had no idea you were workin' here. This is mighty embarrassin'! See, uhhh…back when I was havin' all them problems at my old place I started smokin' the pot, calmed th' nerves, y'know?" Charles drawls on for a bit and I fall asleep in my brain.

"Anyway, here's th' Court Order, just says I gotta take this here class and then I'm a free man!"

I review the Court order and it looks like Charles is telling the truth. Driving under the influence with a joint in his hand, a plea of no contest, and a kindly judge who is worried about jailing a man with a heart condition.

"Well, I guess welcome to the class, Charles." I reach out my hand to shake his and instantly regretted it. I'm sure his hand is clean but now mine feels like I dipped it in bacon grease. "I just have to warn you, while you are in my class you are not my neighbor, you are my student. For the next 12 weeks, we are really going to have to keep some boundaries. We can be friends again after that, alright?"

"Sure thing, boss!" Was Charles' reply. With that, I open the door and start a new class. I expect it to go the same as normal, but Charles is quick to respond to questions and his southern charm appears to win over the class. At the end of the class, I am surprised to see more than a few smiles and head nods on the way out. Somehow, I'm suddenly a good teacher.

Chapter 3

Life continues as normal, a couple nerve-wracking classes a week and Charles stays away from my children and my home as discussed. He still creeps me out, every time I look out the window to check on my kids I can see him sitting on his porch, his liver-spotted face watching them play.

"Oh leave it alone, Shaun! He's a sweet old man. His daughter's passing really took a toll on the old guy. Every time we've spoken, he tells me about it. He even said Brodie reminds him of her so much he's almost moved to tears when he looks at her." Dominique is getting used to my offhand comments about Charles, but she has a big heart and a love for everyone she meets. That's probably why she loves me so much.

"I feel bad for him, and I think he's harmless" was almost a mantra at this point. Hearing that perspective does help calm me from being over-vigilant and sitting in the front lawn with my children and the shotgun I don't own. Maybe he is sincere. Maybe the kids' jovial play helps him feel his daughter is still alive somehow. Who knows, but it isn't quite as easy for me to empathize at this point.

On the evening of Charles' twelfth and last class, I show up almost excited. Mostly I am glad I won't have to deal with Charles anymore, and am hopeful he will leave me and my family alone out of habit. I do have some reservation, however, as the class may return to its original state of apathy and ignoring everything I say.

I sit at the front door and greet each of the convicted drug users, take their money. At 6:00 p.m. I check the roster and notice there is no Charles on my list.

"Where the hell is Charles?" I ask rhetorically.

"No clue, but this is gonna be a lame-ass class without him!" Someone responds, which elicits a large amount of giggles.

I ignore the banter and start the class. The class is surprisingly pleasant without Charles to encourage them. Apparently, a rapport can be built over time. The class laughs at my jokes on occasion and even provide semi-insightful answers. I am so pleased with the result I completely forget Charles' absence.

Chapter 4

After class, I drive home in a cheery mood, humming along to my favorite Rozz Williams song. When I pull into my driveway, I notice my son, Nivek, is playing basketball by himself.

"Hey Nivek! Brodie inside?" I ask with a smile on my face.

"No…Brodie went to Uncle Charles' house. Hesaidhemadeheraspecialcake! He wouldn't share with me though!" Nivek huffs a bit and asks if I will play basketball. I am not paying attention, however. The second I heard the words *Uncle Charles* my heart stops.

A sudden ringing dominates every sound in the world as I turn toward Charles' house. The lights in his house are dim. Every step I take toward Charles' house amplifies the beat of my heart. The ringing in my ears wars with my heartbeat until my heartbeat is a deafening roar. I knock on the door until my knuckles are sore.

Charles answers the door, looking every bit the kindly old man he portends to be. "Hey, Mr. Shaun! How're ya doin? Sorry I missed class I was so busy a'bakin' this cake for yer daughter! She only just got here, mind if I send her home in a bit?"

"BRODIE! GET OUT HERE NOW!" I yell past Charles' onslaught of words. Brodie, for her part, appears rather calm and walks around Charles with an innocent look on her face.

"But Daddy, I didn't get any cake yet!" She quietly complains.

I grab my daughter by her arm and give Charles a

withering look. "Stay the hell away from my family, you hear me, Charles?"

Charles raises his hands and backs away. "Didn't mean no offense, Mr. Shaun, I was jus' tryin' ta be nice, she's such a sweetheart!"

"Stay the hell away." I repeat as I turn my back and walk home with my daughter.

The next fifteen to twenty minutes are consumed with lectures from Dominique and me toward my children. We had both explained our concerns about Charles and strangers in general. The children have their best *we care about what you are saying* faces on, but then I notice Brodie's face starting to droop.

"Brodie? What's wrong, baby?" I ask, suddenly concerned at the lack of expression of her face.

Brodie doesn't respond; she just slumps back into the couch and the drool I hadn't noticed before drips off her cheek.

"Oh my god!" Dominique exclaims.

I immediately move toward my daughter and try everything from pleading, loud words, and even a slap to the face. Brodie is completely unresponsive. I feel for a heartbeat and it's there but it seems too slow. I immediately call 911 to let them know we are driving to the hospital, then I grab my beautiful daughter and run.

Chapter 5

The workers at the Emergency room are able to stabilize Brodie. The doctor on staff enters and opens his clipboard casually.

"So her bloodwork shows she may have ingested too much cough medicine. We see this sometimes, children drinking it by mistake or parents overmedicating. Did she have a cold?" The Doctor asks, looking inquisitively over his clipboard.

"No, she..." Dominique starts to shakily respond.

"Leave it," I whisper in her ear. "Yes, sir. She has had a cold. She must have found the chewable tablets on the table or maybe Dominique and I double dosed her by mistake."

Dominique gives me a concerned look, but apparently trusts my judgment. The doctor continues to talk, but I can't hear anything. All I can hear is the swirling rage in my head. *Charles did this.* Over and over again. I stand up abruptly and stalk out of the room while the Doctor is still talking. I can hear people calling for me but I don't take notice. My mind is no longer able to rationalize outside voices.

Charles did this.

I numbly get into my car and drive to my work. I unlock the door with shaking hands, not from fear, but from anger-inspired adrenalin. *Charles did this.* I open the drawer to my desk, pull out the three-month-old Molly, and crush it into a powder. *Charles did this.* I drive numbly back to my house, park, and enter my home.

Dominique has a stash of marijuana from before we dated, I found it while I was cleaning one day and I pretended not to notice. Now I'm glad I found it. I open the bag and cover the acrid green substance with the crushed Molly.

I don't remember walking to Charles' house but now I am knocking on his door. Charles answers and looks surprised. "Shaun? What's wrong?" He asks, a little too casually.

"Nothing, Charles, nothing at all. I just wanted to apologize for how I acted earlier. You would not believe how excited Brodie was, and how easily she went down tonight! She is usually up for hours. I have been giving it some thought and realize you've just been a huge help to me and the family, so I wanted to congratulate you on passing the class! I already sent the certificate of completion to your probation officer!" I say, feeling every ounce of enthusiasm but for all the wrong reasons.

Charles initially looks confused, but then looks excited. He invites me in and I enter his house. I say generous things, praising his décor and his help with my class. When I pull out the marijuana, Charles looks startled and defensive.

"Sorry, I looked through the house, I don't drink beer, and this was all we had! A counselor can't have a little fun sometimes?" I ask.

Charles appears pleased by my statement and pulls out a pipe from his side table. He packs his bowl and takes a few hits, coughs, compliments my offering, and passes the bowl. I reciprocate by taking as small a hit as possible. I cough until I feel like my soul will fall out of my face. Charles laughs appreciatively and gladly takes back the bowl. I can already feel my heart rate speeding up from the Molly.

Charles takes another few hits. When he hands back the bowl I can tell he is shaking.

"Some mighty strong stuff you…you…got here…Not sure I been this high in…" Charles compliments as he grabs his chest and looks confused.

I am ready for this. I wait for him to fall to the ground and then I pull out my CPR kit. I put the mouth protector (so you don't have to touch mouths when resuscitating someone) and make sure to take a puff off the bowl before I provide Charles with each breath of life--or in this case, death.

With each Molly-tainted breath of life, I sit back up to watch Charles' liver-spotted face. He is in a panic and trying to move. But I am sitting on him, holding his arms. Every time he gasps for air, I give him another mouthful of the laced marijuana. I am thankful for the CPR training I received prior to my internship as I watch his eyes transition from fear, panic, and then utter lifelessness.

"Don't ever touch my fucking daughter again," I say, as I walk out of the dead man's house.

The End

By Shaun Phelps

Facebook Zombie Book of The Month Club

Zombie Stories for People with Short Attention Spans

Made in the USA
Coppell, TX
01 May 2020